Family Ties, Missing Organs, & Champagne

An Anna Romano Mystery Series

Book Three

Cheryl Denise Bannerman

PRINT ISBN: 978-1-7353352-6-1

This is a work of fiction. All of the characters, names, incidents, organizations, and dialogue in this novel are either the products of the author's imagination or are used fictitiously.

Table of Contents

CHAPTER 1

Once Upon a Happily Ever After

Anna

O nce upon a time there was a young lady, and yes I can say 'young', who lived with her seven cats and was a very successful mystery author. One day, in the middle of a horrible kidnapping case, she met a handsome detective. (Quick sidebar: I can't say what one thing it was that caught my eye, but he had the most captivating features. Six foot four, lean and in shape, but not too muscular, with these intense green eyes that a girl could get lost in.) Anyway, after dating for several months, the young lady and handsome detective fell in love and moved in together. All of her cats loved him and soon they were living happily ever after.

In case you are just joining in on the fun, my name is Anna Romano, and that 'once upon a time' story was about me.

But, who am I kidding, that stuff just happens in books and movies, right? Well, actually, I'm kind of living the fairytale now. John and I are getting along great and my babies do love him. So, what's my complaint? I guess it would be that John works too much. I mean, I love the freedom and space he gives me to write and attend all of my author events, but I would like to spend more time with him.

Today is an exception. Albeit, it's a normal day for me, picking up cat litter, groceries, and soil from the local nursery; but for John, it's a day of NOT solving murders and napping peacefully on a mild, breezy afternoon. It's been many months since I accidentally stumbled upon those two dead bodies in the Atkinson case, and everyone has gone on with their lives. Even though Chatty Cathy messaged me for weeks after the case was closed, pestering me for a new story, I've managed to stay out of trouble. Moreover, my book about the Atkinson case, *A Killer Charity Ball to Die For*, was a bestseller, which my publicist, Shirlene, was very happy about.

However, as I head back home with the windows down, enjoying the sunshine, the cool breeze, and a bag of cheetos, while listening to a soft rock station, I can't help but wonder what excitement lies ahead. You know what they say about the 'calm before the storm'.

As I pull up to the house, I see Ms. Martinez and Mr. Craigly smiling and laughing in front of his house and TatorTot, my Persian, sitting in the window waiting for me, and smile to myself.

It seems as if love is in the air. Life is good.

CHAPTER 2

Itching for Attention...and a Nap

John

Today is quite the luxury, a day off. I'm laying on the couch, enjoying a cannoli, and flicking through channels on the TV. It doesn't happen often, that's for sure. But when it does, it's pure heaven.

The past few months have actually been kind of peaceful. Anna has not stumbled upon any dead bodies recently, nor has she tried to maneuver herself into the middle of my murder investigations, and I'm left to do my detective work on my own. Just the way I like it.

I'm very pleased with our living arrangement and have actually grown quite fond of her babies. Waking up to Anna's sweet face every morning is wonderful. And, of course, her cooking is phenomenal. What more could a man ask for? It's the perfect life, for now. The 'M' word hasn't come up yet; but, I'm sure it will soon.

Anna is off doing her normal shopping routine and I was going to enjoy a nap, but then I thought about those cannoli in the frigerator. And Tiny and Petra were itching for some attention, so I lost track of time. Just when I was about to hunker down, the phone rang. It was my parents.

"Mom, Dad, how are you? Is everything okay?" I asked.

"Yes, everything is fine. Can't we just call to see how you and Anna are doing? Why does there have to be an ulterior motive?" they responded, almost talking over each other. And, I can imagine both of them crowded together around the speaker phone on the kitchen wall.

I was already suspicious. Perhaps it's just a hazard of the job. For the next thirty minutes, they went on and on about how Anna and I are not getting any younger and we need to make a decision about the next step in our relationship. Then the conversation moved on to their desire for grandchildren. I can't believe I'm saying this, but I'd much rather be playing with the cats right now than endure this conversation. As if on cue, Petra jumps at the phone, like she's trying to swipe it out of my hands. I whisper a stern 'stop!' and pointed a serious finger, and she curls up on my belly purring.

"I'll be sure to discuss all of this with Anna and get back to you. Thank you so much for calling," I faltered, trying to get them off the phone and go back to my lazy day off.

"One more thing before you go, sweetie," my mother added in a loving voice. "Your father and I think it would be a good idea if you spent more time with your brother. You know how much he looks up to you."

Looks up to me? Despises me, more like, for getting my life together and joining the force, while he continued his life of crime. Running around, getting into trouble, is fun when you're in high school, but once it goes past twenty-five, it's just pathethic. I'm tired of bailing Scott out of 'this predicament' or 'that debt' every few months. I wish Mom and Dad would just wash their hands of him, once and for all. They deserve to enjoy their retirement in peace. Let Scott dig himself out of whatever hole he has dug this time and straighten out his own life.

Just then, I heard a tap at the front door. Tiny was the first one to leap from the couch to the foyer. Anna peeked her head in and gestured she needed help with the bags. This was just the escape I needed.

"You're absolutely right! I will definitely try to do that. But, I'm afraid I have to cut this short, Anna needs my help bringing in some bags of soil from the car. You know how much she loves her gardening. Can I call you guys back later ?" I bargained.

I didn't wait for their reply and hurried off the phone as quick as I could, without being disrespectful, of course.

I slipped on my shoes and headed out to the car to carry the bags from the trunk. Anna was engrossed in a conversation across the street with Ms. Martinez and Mr. Craigly. I smiled and waved as I unloaded the trunk and headed back inside.

With the groceries unpacked, and Anna settling back into her gardening, I grabbed a beer from the fridge and headed back to the couch to finish enjoying my day off. I settled on an old western on TV and eventually drifted off to sleep.

CHAPTER 3

Heavy Drinking and a DV Charge

Scott

Everybody just needs to chill. Always on my back about getting my life together, as if I'm purposely messing up. I *am* trying.

After I got out of jail, I met a woman, and she helped me get a job at a local hardware store. So, I spend most of my days helping mostly old guys find tools, screws, and lawncare machinery. It's boring, but it's a job.

But, a couple of weeks ago I lost the job. It seems the owner doesn't appreciate two-hour lunches that include Scotch. Whatever.

Needless to say, my old lady is not happy. She's been hounding me about getting another job ever since.

Oh, I forgot to tell you about Tess, my old lady. She's great. Met her the day I got out of the joint on some trumped-up fraud charges. She was standing on the sidewalk admiring a dress in some lady's boutique window. She was cute, tall, blonde, curvy in all the right places, just the way I like my women. I walked up to her and said in my smoothest cassanova voice, "You would look absolutely stunning in that dress. You should buy it."

She flashed me a big, bright smile with perfect, white teeth and blushed, mumbled something about the cost on a TA's salary and asked me my name. She was a real straight-shooter and I liked that in a woman. We hit it off right away and she didn't care about my past, just about what I was planning for the future. She invited me to move in pretty quickly after we started dating. Tess made me want to be a better man and I wanted to make her proud. But…with me there is always a but. The pressure of being responsible for another person, paying rent and bills, was overwhelming. And when I am overwhelmed, I drink.

I know I'm not supposed to be fratenizing with the boys from the joint, but any other friends I used to have are long gone, meaning dead or still in jail. I needed to be around people who understood me and my lifestyle.

So, one long lunch turned into five 'happy hours' after work per week, and bar hopping on the weekends, and so on, and so on.

This morning I woke up with a hangover from being out all night drinking with the boys, and Tess was in a mood. I barely got both of my eyes open when she started in on me. Turns out it was actually afternoon and she wanted to know why my lazy, good-for-nothing butt had been wasting the day away in bed, when I should have been up checking the Sunday papers for employment.

I could still hear the pounding in my head over the yelling. "This is way more than I bargained for, Scott! What happened to the man I met, who was so determined to turn his life around and make a fresh start?" she asked. "You have no income, all you do is hang out drinking with the boys!"

Honestly, I don't know where 'that man' went, but I'm sure he'll be back soon. Just then my phone chimed, as if on cue. I lifted the phone from the nightstand and quickly glanced at the screen; I had a message. I tried to place it face down again without looking startled, but Tess misses nothing.

"Who was that?" she demanded.

"Just one of the boys, it's nothing."

I guess my facial expression and the pitch in my voice gave it away, because she reached for the phone on the nightstand in lightening speed and read the message. I just waited for the bomb to go off.

"What the hell is this? 'Thanks for last night' from some unknown number. Thanks for what, Scott?! Who were you with? Did you cheat on me? Because I swear if cheated on me…" she threatened.

Before she could finish, I jumped out of bed and attempted to straighten her out. "Of course not! I would never cheat on you! I don't know who this person is and what they are 'thanking' me for, I swear, Tess!" I contended.

She was at her wits' end, and between the loss of income, the drinking, and the mysterious text message, I knew the next words out of her mouth would be bad news. She wanted some space. But, where the hell would I go?

It wasn't that I didn't understand why. I mean, the arguments were getting worse and worse, and sometimes physical. Last week, Tess just missed my head when she threw a plate at the wall. The last thing I need is a domestic violence (aka DV) charge on my sheet while I'm still on probation. I'd immediately get thrown back in the joint!

I turned to the only people I knew would never turn their back on me. Frank and Esther Solace.

"Hey, Mom, how are you?" I was trying to sound happy.

"I'm just fine, son. Hold on, let me get your father on the line."

I waited while they fussed back and forth, trying to get the speaker phone in the kitchen to work properly.

A few minutes later, they were both on the line. Dad was the first to speak. "So, what's going on this time, Scott?" he asked solemnly.

My mother chimed in quickly, "Now, let's not jump to conclusions, Frank. Scott may be just calling to tell us how well he's doing with Tess and the new job. Right, Scott?"

I hesitated. "Well, actually, Mom, Tess and I have been fighting a lot lately." I took a deep breath and summoned up the courage to continue. "You see, I lost the job at the hardware store and had a few drinks with the boys, and now she says she wants her space for a little while. I just don't know what to do or where to go…"

Dad was silent, so my mom spoke up. "I was afraid of this, based on our last phone call. And, Tess is such a nice girl. But, don't worry son, I know just the person you should call!"

It was the last name on earth I would have ever thought she would suggest.

Cat Naps and Kisses

Anna

"**T**hanks for helping unload the trunk, sweetie," I said, as I got on my tippy toes and kissed him on the cheek. John grabbed me up and enveloped me in a big bear hug and began nuzzling my neck with kisses.

I quickly retreated, "Oh no you don't. I have gardening to finish, mister. Now go back to your lazy day of rest on the couch."

We both laughed and went our separate ways for the afternoon.

I decided to use my new cell phone bluetooth gadget to call my publicist, Shirlene, before I was up to my elbows in soil.

"Well, if it isn't the 'lone detective'! How the heck are ya? Staying out of trouble, I hope?" she asked, before I could even get to say 'hello'.

"Well, actually, I've been out of the murder investigative business for quite some time now, for your information." This was partially true anyway. "I've been staying out of trouble and out of John's work since the Atkinson case, but who knows what the future holds."

"Amazing! I'm sure John is elated! Sorry, I haven't had a minute to Skype with you, but I've been distracted with a new romance of my own. The gentleman from the editor's conference I told you about. Anyway, enough about me, how are things with you and John?"

She was purposely changing the subject before I had a chance to respond. I'll get on her later for more details about this mysterious gentleman. I responded, "Great! I'm actually content for once in my life. You'll be happy to know he has officially moved in and is subletting his apartment." I beamed proudly.

"No way! I can't believe it! Do I hear wedding bells in the future?" Shirlene asked slyly.

"Not to say I haven't thought about it, but no. Although, I heard John on the phone with his parents this afternoon when I came in, and they were already pushing the 'm' word and looking for grandchildren. Ugh."

"Wow! They sound pushier than me! Well, you know, the big four-oh is approaching, so maybe you should give it some more thought, you know?"

I was about to give her a piece of my mind about the age thing when the house phone rang. I told her I would call her back and disconnected, trying to grab the cordless before it woke John, who was snoring softly on the couch with Petra on his chest and Tiny at his feet.

Although the sight was adorable and he needed the rest, it was Scott on the line and he sounded frantic.

Reluctantly, I proceeded to nudge John gently to wake him up.

CHAPTER 5

Groveling Doesn't Become Me

Scott

John sounds half asleep when he picks up. Great, now he's going to be extra cranky and mean. Why did I listen my parents about asking him for a place to stay? I wanted to just hang up.

"Hellooooo! Scott? You there?" John was speaking loudly, already frustrated with me.

"Bro, heyyyy! Sorry about that, bad connection. How's it going?"

"Well, I was kind of trying to enjoy my day off and catch up on some sleep. What's up?" John asked.

"Well, you see, Mom and Dad, well they thought…um," I stuttered. I was struggling to find the right words. It was just like when we were young. John was always the one with the good grades and good looks. I remember Mom and Dad fussing over him all the time, especially when he would speak at auditorium events and play lead roles in the school plays. Other parents would say, "Oh, he's so well-spoken and well-mannered."

Nevermind the fact that during our teenage years, he was right beside me wreaking havoc on the neighborhood. Those were the good ole days, man. Nothing major, but just bullying the nerds, pranks, and stealing a few bikes here and there.

As if intruding on my thoughts, John's booming voice breaks in. "Just spit it out, Scott! What mess have you gotten yourself into now?"

"Okay, so here it is…"

I go through the entire story, since I got out of jail to the last argument with Tess. "So, basically, Mom and Dad said I should reach out to you and see if I can stay there for a few weeks, just while Tess cools off. She says not to come back until I have a steady income in place. What do you say, Bro?"

After a long pause, John launched his usual speech. "They what? No way! I knew you couldn't straighten out your life. You could have been given some hard time with this last conviction of credit card fraud! Do you understand? You're lucky I was able to put in a good word for you with the DA. When are you going to learn? You'll never grow up! You know you're killing Mom and Dad?"

"I know, Bro, I know. I'm really trying. This is the last time, I swear," I pleaded.

"Scott, this is not even my home. I have to discuss this with Anna. I'll call you back."

The line disconnected.

Whew! That went a lot better than I thought it would.

CHAPTER 6

Beggars Can't Be Choosy

John

Anna was right. Scott did sound frantic. Apparently, he is up to his old ways again and his live-in girlfriend isn't having it. I told Mom and Dad, a leopard never changes its spots.

How much more disappointment can they take?

I couldn't believe what I was hearing, he actually wants to stay HERE for a couple of weeks. So this is what my parents were hinting at.

I told him I had to discuss it with Anna and call him back.

Anna was just coming in the house from the garden. She was headed to the kitchen to wash her hands as I approached her, hesitantly. "You will never believe what that was about."

But before she could respond, the house phone rang again. It was my parents. They wanted to make one last plea for me to take Scott in, by trying to 'guilt' me into 'saving' my younger brother from himself. I gave my usual response that a person has to want help and want to change, in order to make a change in their life.

Once again, I disconnected respectfully, agreeing to talk to Anna as soon as possible.

I hung up and Anna was standing behind me drying her hands on a dish towel with a crease of concern etched in her forehead. She was obviously wondering what was going on.

I explained. "Well, dear, it seems my parents think I am a saviour of sorts. They want me to step in and save my brother from himself…again."

"Oh, I see," Anna replied slowly.

"They want to know if he can stay here for a few weeks, and if I can pull some strings and help him get a job back in

Newark, so he can move back in with Tess with some kind of income."

After a few moments of contemplation, turning off the television, wiping the kitchen counter and sweeping up some litter, she responded.

She says he can stay in the guest room above the garage for *no more than three weeks*. It has a fully functioning bathroom, so he won't have to disturb us, except for food.

I give her another bear hug and tell her she's the greatest girlfriend ever. I was wondering to myself if I would ever say 'greatest wife ever' when the phone rang again.

This time it was Scott and my parents. He had conferenced them in and they were still 'oohing and aahing', fascinated by the technology, when I picked up. I told them what our decision was and held my ear away from the phone while they praised and thanked me.

I truly hope I do not regret this decision.

CHAPTER 7

To Stay or Not to Stay...Said the Houseguest

Anna

Well, today's the day. Yikes. I wish I could say I'm okay about it, but to be honest I'm nervous *— as nervous as I was when I submitted the first manuscript to a publishing company.* My stomach is in knots. I've never met his brother and what I do know about him is not exactly flattering. What if he's dangerous? Although, I'm sure John would not have entertained the idea of him coming here if he was. He's too protective of me.

John and I offered to pick him up from the bus station, but he said he would take an Uber. I'm busying myself in the kitchen, while John burns a hole in the living room carpet by pacing back and forth. Apparently, Tiny thinks it's a game, so he stays close on his heels trying to tap the top of his slippers with his paw. Sonny, Liza and Bette are obviously taking score, their little, furry heads whipping back and forth as if they were watching a tennis match.

I decided this was a special occasion, so I'm making ricotta and egg gnocchi with olives, capers, and tomato Sauce. (See Appendix for recipe) I was just , peeling the potatoes and passing them through the potato ricer into a bowl, when John pokes his head into the kitchen.

He tells me Scott is out front.

I dash to the front window and can already imagine what the nosy neighbors will be saying. My life could literally be a reality show with all the chaos, drama and unusual characters, *including me.* Ha! I look out to see a tall, handsome, blond-haired man step out of the car with a large, blue duffle bag slung over his shoulder. I was expecting him to have dark brown hair like John, so the long, blonde, unruly mane was quite a shock. He has features like their mother, while John takes after their father. Both had strong jawlines and deep-set eyes, except his eyes were blue.

He turned to wave the driver off and headed up the sidewalk, while brushing the hair from his eyes. Sporting a t-shirt and ripped jeans, he had a lazy gait as if he hadn't a care in the world *—which was far from the truth.*

John opened the door and greeted his brother with a brief hug and led him in the house. I could see Mr. Craigly, head of the neighborhood watch, peeking through his window to get a better look at the stranger, *coming to wreak havoc on his quiet neighborhood*, was what I'm sure he was thinking.

I wiped my hands on my apron and opened my arms to embrace our guest. "Scott! Welcome! It's so nice to finally meet you. How was your trip?"

"Well, thanks, uh Anna. It was good, thanks. You have a great house! Can't say I've ever bunked in such a rich neighborhood, or even in Princeton, for that matter. You guys near the university?"

"Well, yes, it's right…" I started, but was cut off by John.

"Nevermind that, college girls should be the last thing on your mind. And you won't be staying here necessarily. Anna has a room above the garage. We'll get you settled in a minute, but first I need to lay down some ground rules," John said, sternly.

Scott stood there frozen, not sure how to respond. I could tell he was a bit intimidated by his older brother.

"John, where are your manners. He just got here. Can I offer you something to drink, Scott?" I asked. I noticed none of my babies went near him, they just circled him, checking him out.

John rolled his eyes and stood there with his arms folded across his chest.

"I'm fine for now, thanks. I'm used to big brother laying down the law. Frankly, I don't how you put up with him," he chuckled. But John was not laughing. I've never seen him this serious. I was sure their relationship was strained, but I didn't think the family dynamic would be this tense.

"Nevermind that, let's just get to it," John replied.

I headed back into the kitchen to check on dinner while John provided him with the password to the wifi, the arrangements he made with his probation officer, the no drinking or drugs rule, and the fact that he could come down to the house for meals.

During the day, Scott will continue his community service and attend his required AA meetings. Everything was closeby, so he could walk or catch the bus.

I was rolling the dough for gnocchis when John and Scott passed by, no doubt headed out the front to the staircase that led to Scott's room.

I yelled after them, "Dinner's at 6 o'clock sharp, Scott! I left some fresh towels in your bathroom!"

"Thanks, Anna!" he called back.

He seemed like a nice enough guy, but I can't help shake the feeling that he was not only running from Tess and his responsibilities, but something else altogether.

I was just putting the dough in the fridge to chill, when my cell phone rang. Seeing the caller ID, I picked it up with a smile. "Why don't you ever call the house phone first? You know I'm home, if I'm not out with you."

Shirlene laughed, "I don't know that! You could have a secret best friend in Princeton I don't know about!"

We laughed for a moment, and she continued, "I just want to make sure you are all set for this weekend."

"Absolutely!" I exclaimed.

The book event had been planned for months. I'd have to be a fool to pass up a book signing in a major bookstore in sunny Florida.

"Okay, just checking. I know how you hate leaving John home alone to fend for himself. God forbid he has to make his own meals. Geez!" Shirlene joked.

"True. But, not this time. We have a house guest."

"A house guest? Who?" she asked.

I explained the situation with John's brother, Scott's troubles, and the tension between the two.

"Wow, too much family drama for me."

"Yeah, it's okay though. I just think they need some time to talk and work things out, maybe even bond like brothers again. It's been a while since they saw each other," I explained.

Shirlene agreed and preceded to tell me the time and place to meet her on Saturday, and not to be late, before hanging up.

Thank goodness the publishing company is sending a car to pick me up for the airport. I only had a day to pack, so I'd better get started tonight. I already had the PERFECT sunflower sundress picked out for the event and I can already feel the Florida sunshine on my skin.

CHAPTER 8

A Full Schedule...and Stomach

John

It's only been thirty minutes since my brother arrived and I'm already stressed. Even though we spoke a few months ago, it's been fifteen years since we last physically saw each other. A lot of emotions are flooding my mind right now, ranging from anxiety to happiness. I'm happy to see him, but I know he hasn't changed or grown up since we were teens, and everywhere he goes, trouble is not far behind. Getting into trouble was fun as a teen, but once I hit my 20s it started to wear on me. Scott never forgave me for getting my life together and, in his words, "abandoning" him.

I stepped in the front door and headed for the kitchen. "Smells good, sweetheart. I reminded Scott to come down around six."

Anna nodded as she put the finishing touches on the sauce. I could tell she was holding her tongue, so I started setting the table. Finally, I blurted out, "Go ahead, just say it, Anna."

"Say what?" she answered coyly.

"You know what. I know that face. And when *you're* silent, there's definitely a problem."

She turned from the stove and looked at me with those sexy, brown eyes and flowing brown hair that seductively fell over her right eye. She tossed her head back and swiped it away from her face before she spoke. "Now John, dear, you know how much I care for you and your family. I know you and your brother have a history and some of it is not pleasant…"

"I hear a 'but' coming," I interjected.

"But, it seems like he is really trying to get his act together. Can't you lighten up on him a little bit? Maybe, spend this weekend trying to reconnect with him while I'm away?" Anna pleaded.

I couldn't argue with Anna. I was like putty in her hands. I sidled over to her and hugged her. "I'll try. But, only because you asked so nicely."

She returned to the stove and I finished setting the table with the salad, Italian bread, and tub of margarine.

"Did you show Scott where everything was and give him the key?" she asked.

"Yep. He's taking a shower now," I responded. "And, I also told him where he will be reporting to for his community service on Monday."

I was looking forward to being alone this weekend. Anna and I have never been apart for that long since I moved in, and this trip actually extended past the weekend until Tuesday. As if reading my mind, she asked,"Will you miss me while I'm gone, Detective?"

"Well, I'll definitely miss your cooking!" I said aloud with an animated smile while rolling my eyes.

Anna threw a dish towel at me from across the room and we both joked and laughed like a couple of teenagers. I love what we have together. It's just comes so naturally.

We were discussing the time her ride was arriving Saturday morning when Scott walked in.

It was a dinner full of childhood stories, police stories, and stories of my mystery escapades. Even without the wine, which I put away before Scott arrived, it was a dinner full of laughter and smiles. By the end of the night, Scott and I were finishing dessert and loosening the top button of our pants because we had eaten too much. Anna had left us in the living room watching action movies, as she turned in for the night.

Maybe this could be a second chance for me and Scott.

A second chance to reconnect as brothers.

* * *

It's been a long two days so far without Anna. Sleeping and waking up alone under the rose-patterned comforter with Tiny and Petra at my feet, and Liza and Bette asleep on the floor below, was some comfort, but not much. But, you know what they say... absence makes the heart grow fonder. We text during the day and have our nightly call where we blow kisses and make that smoochy sound into the phone. One night, we tried video chat from the laptop in the living room and the cats hogged up the entire call! Thank goodness her trip is almost over.

I have to admit, though, it had been nice spending time with Scott this past weekend. When I wasn't on duty, we went to the movies and spent time at the batting cages. We used to love that when we were kids. He still had quite an arm on him with a bat speed of 70 mph.

The only thing I made since Anna has been gone was coldcut sandwiches, but it was good enough for Scott. He hasn't gotten 'spoiled' by Anna's cooking just yet.

Scott actually opened up and told me all about Tess. He really seems to care about her and wants things to work out. I also shared a little about my future plans with Anna, if she'll have me.

My connection managed to russle up a good lead for Scott when he returns to Newark. It's not too far from where he is staying with Tess, over at Seton Hall University doing janitorial work.

While I had the rare opportunity to sleep in until eight this morning, Scott had to wake up by six and should already be headed to the municipal building for community service. There was a shuttle bus waiting to take everyone to the park, where they would start the first cleanup project. I'll check with the supervisor over there later to see how things are going and if he was on time.

After feeding the babies and cleaning the litter boxes, I showered and got ready for work. The silence was annoying and I decided to head to the coffee shop for breakfast. I tried a caramel latte this morning with a double shot of expresso, just to be different. Without Anna, my appetite wasn't as big, so breakfast was just a toasted and buttered croissant.

I arrived to the station about the same time as Billings and we walked through the double glass doors together. I was just about to ask him how his date went the night before when my cell phone rang. I saw the caller ID and smiled, then ducked over to the corner of the lobby to take the call.

"How's my rosebud this morning?"

"Wonderful! How's my handsome detective this morning? Surviving okay without me, I hope?"

"Barely. I can't wait for you to get back."

"Me too. Although I must say, I am enjoying the sunshine state of Florida *immensely.* We HAVE TO come back and vacation here. My goodness, you would love it!"

"I'm assuming the event went well?"

"Oh yeah, the first part of the book signing and mystery novel convention went great. Today is the meet and greet that the publisher set up to discuss my next book."

"I see. Well, that sounds good. You know, you haven't shared any hints about that with me yet. There isn't a murder going on that I don't know about, is there?" I inquired suspiciously.

"Of course not, dear. I would never investigate a murder case without you!" Anna chuckled.

I rolled my eyes, knowing that was only half true and said, "Yes, dear. So what time does your flight come in tomorrow?"

"Around two in the afternoon, but I know you'll be at work, so the publishing company already arranged for a car to bring me home from the airport."

"Sounds good, we'll chat later tonight then?" I asked.

"Absolutely. Toodles!"

I smiled at her theatrics and headed to my desk. One day very soon our phone conversations will end differently. It's not that I didn't 'love' her, I just hadn't mustered up the courage to say it to anyone since Martha died.

And, what if she didn't feel the same way, or say it back to me?

I guess I'll never know until I try.

CHAPTER 9

Home Sweet Home

Anna

"**A**hhhhh, home sweet home," I sighed as I approached the front door of my home. It was gray skies here in Jersey and a chilly fall day – a stark difference from sunny, hot, and humid Florida. This was my home for almost 15 years, with a garden and white picket fence, and all of my babies. I'm looking through the window at Petra and Sonny fighting aggressively for my attention, and, in doing so, knocking over the spider plant I had propped on my sill. Ugh.

I pulled out my key and let myself in, immediately scolding the two instigators who made the mess on the floor, and started cleaning up the soil.

Afterwards, I headed to bedroom to drop off my luggage, plopped on the bed, and looked around the room. Not too bad, but you could tell John is a recently transformed bachelor. Ha! Clothes scattered here and there, on the floor and on top of the hamper (as if lifting the lid and putting the items inside was too much trouble), and a few cups on the dresser. I was drowning in cat hair and loud purring, while all my babies showed me how much they had missed me. I pulled out my phone to text John I was home. The message was full of mushy phrases and lots of emoticons, and he responded with lots of hearts.

I thought about heading to the kitchen to make a special dinner for him and Scott, but instead, made a u-turn in the hallway to take a quick shower. After spending the entire flight back next to an elderly man with what sounded like a combo of strep throat and whooping cough, I figured I couldn't be too careful.

When I felt like the germs were washed away, I stepped out and dried off, wrapping another towel around my head like a turban.

Next, I texted Shirlene to let her know I arrived home safely. She replied with a smart remark about the flight back and the whooping cough man. I was not amused.

Now, to start my special dinner. Since I had some olives, capers and anchovy fillets in the fridge, I decided to make spaghetti alla puttanesca. (See Appendix for recipe) I heat my oil in a large pot over medium heat. Next, I add garlic and let it sit for minute, before I add my peeled tomatoes into the puree with basil, Kalamata olives, anchovies, capers, oregano, and crushed red pepper. Now, to let that simmer over medium-low heat until it's thickened. I'll make the pasta and salad a bit later, closer to when John is set to come home, around six . I texted him to pick up a baguette on the way home.

I had some time to spare, so I decided to check in on Scott and see if he was back from community service yet. I headed out the front door and walked towards the garage, when I hear Mr. Craigly on his motor scooter coming up the sidewalk behind me.

"Ms. Romano," he said grumpily.

I kept walking, as if I was deep in thought, or suddenly hard of hearing, hoping to reach the steps to Scott's room before he called me again.

"Ms. Romano!" he barked.

I turned around slowly. "Mr. Craigly, how are you? I didn't hear you come up behind me," I lied, resisting the urge to roll my eyes.

"What do you have, some type of bed and breakfast going on here?" he demanded.

"Why would you say that?"

"I saw yet *another* man coming and going. And, it wasn't the detective guy."

"You mean John. Anyway, it's his brother. He's staying with us for a bit."

"Well, this is a respectable community. Since he's been here, I've seen several seedy characters around."

"I'm sure you're mistaken, Mr. Craigly. You know I'm making spaghetti alla puttanesca this evening. You're welcome to join us for dinner."

"Hmph. Don't think you can change the subject!" he replied. After a short pause he asked, "Is that the dish with the olives and capers?"

"It sure is. See you around seven!" I waved and continued up the steps. Thank goodness he could always be bribed with food. He was especially cranky today, though. And, I wonder what he meant by seedy characters hanging around.

Before I knocked, I turned to see him zoom off across the street on his motor scooter to our other nosy neighbor, Ms. Martinez. Probably to talk about about me.

Ms. Martinez is the neighborhood gossip and mixed with the neighborhood watch guard, Mr. Craigly, the pair are turning out to be a deadly combination.

I rapped on Scott's door a few times and surprisingly, the door inched forward. I know this is a safe neighborhood, but even I don't leave my door open, or unlocked.

"Scott, you here?" I called out.

There was no response, so I pushed the door open further and walked inside. I couldn't believe the state of the room after only a few days. It was a mess! Tables were overturned, there were clothes and other items strewn all over the floor, and there was a putrid smell in the air. I decided I was going to have a serious talk with Scott the next time I see him. This was unacceptable!

I called out his name again and headed towards the bathroom. The door was closed, but no one answered my call, so I thought I'd better check to be sure he's okay.

I put my hands over my eyes and opened the door slowly. "Scott, are you in here? I sure hope you're decent?"

Again, there was no answer and the smell was even worse, so I opened my eyes. The shower curtain was closed and I noticed a dark shadow behind it. I slowly pulled the curtain back to investigate, while covering my mouth and nose from the smell.

"If this is some kind of joke, Scott, it's not funny, and I'm sure John would NOT -" I stopped, mid-sentence.

The next sound that escaped from my mouth was a blood-curdling scream. Lying in the bathtub was a woman. A dead woman. With a gunshot wound to the head and chest, noticeable by the large, round, black holes.

I quickly ran out of the room and down the steps, where Mr. Craigly and Ms. Martinez were rushing towards me on the sidewalk, asking me what was wrong. They had apparently heard me screaming. I hold up my finger, while I fumbled around in my pocket for my cell phone with the other hand, and dialed 911. Afterwards, I dialed John. I could tell he was shocked and confused at the same time, and ordered me to stay put until help arrived.

After I hung up, I stood in silence waiting for the police. It was clear my neighbors were listening to both calls, because they didn't have any questions for me whatsoever, just a look of disbelief and dread on their faces as they tried to comfort me.

CHAPTER 10

Murder In My Home

John

Billings and I were wrapping up a domestic violence case near the university when Anna called. At first, I thought it was a joke, but then dispatch radioed the request a few seconds later. We wrapped up the dispute — *the wife declining to press charges, and the husband leaving to cool off for the night* — and headed towards the house.

The whole time I was driving, I could not figure out where my brother was and who the DB was in his room. Anna didn't say it was Scott, so I assumed he was fine. I tried texting and calling him on his cell, but he wouldn't respond or pick up. It's so typical of Scott. Just like I told everyone, trouble follows him everywhere he goes. Billings was silent the whole ride. He's probably thinking what everyone else in the department was thinking…what are the odds that another murder occurs and Anna is somehow involved AGAIN.

When we pulled up, half the force was already there. I saw Anna on the curb with the neighbors, crying and shaking her head, trying to tell her story to the officers in charge. We would be the talk of the neighborhood for sure after our house is on the news because of a murder. I could hear the HOA complaints now.

I headed straight for Anna, to make sure she's not hurt and ask if she's heard from Scott. She says no and proceeds to tell me about the woman shot twice in the tub. She went up to the room to invite Scott for dinner and found the place was a mess, like it had been ransacked.

"Are you okay if I leave you for a minute? I need to inspect the scene with Billings," I asked Anna, as I wiped a tear from her cheek.

She nodded, so Billings and I headed over to greet the other officers on the scene and start up the steps.

I nodded at the officer posted at the door and walked in. I couldn't believe the mess. Somehow, Scott's troubles in Newark followed him here. CSU hadn't gotten here yet, so there were only a few detectives on the scene. Billings hung back at the front door, while I walked towards the bathroom. The other officers scattered out of respect and let me into the bathroom to view the victim.

Oddly enough, she was fully clothed and soaking wet. I recognized the woman from her photo. It was Tess, Scott's 'old lady', as he often called her. I could tell the shower curtain had been pulled back to expose the body. I'll have to ask the first officer on the scene if it was like that when he arrived, or had he pulled it back. Only her left arm and left leg were lazily hanging over the side of the tub, as if she were thrown in while unconscious. Her head was tilted back against the white tiles and her eyes and mouth were wide open. Blond strands were dangling over the edge of the tub. While I was examining the gun-shot wounds, I noticed the close range of the shot and the scarce amount of blood in the tub or bathroom floor. I'm thinking the killer must have used a silencer. Otherwise, the nosy neighbors would certainly have heard something.

I looked around the bathroom for additional clues, but found nothing more than Scott's shaving kit and toothbrush on the sink. And, certainly, no sign a woman had been staying here.

I was turning to leave when Victor almost knocked me over. I was not in the mood for Victor's 'dude' lingo today.

"Where's the DB, dude?" Victor asked, as if on cue.

I did one of Anna's internal eye rolls and pointed to the tub, and then, asked "Where's the doc?"

"On another murder. Busy night tonight. Bummer this one happening in your own house, though. Like, what are the odds, seriously?"

Before I could wipe that stupid smirk off his face, Carmen walked in with her CSU kit and body bag. I nodded. It was our normal greeting, she likes to keep things formal.

"Hello, detective. If you're finished, we need to get started with processing the scene."

"Of course, can you stop by downstairs, when you have your initial findings?" I asked.

"Downstairs?"

"Yeah, Carmen, I guess you don't know. Um. This is my house… well, er, its Anna's house, you know…where Anna and I live."

Her eyes widened and she began to apologize profusely.

"It's okay, Carmen, I didn't *actually* know the victim. Thanks, though. I'll be downstairs, just ring the bell."

I left them to their work and went to find Anna. I checked my phone while heading down the steps, no new messages or calls from Scott yet. I sent a text to his AA sponsor to see if he had heard from him. Billings met me at the bottom of the steps.

"How's it going in there?" he inquired, concern etched on his face.

"I don't know, Billings. It just doesn't make any sense. The victim is definitely Scott's girl, but how did she get here and why is Scott M.I.A.? Not to mention, it looks horrible for my brother."

I rubbed my temples trying to relieve the pain from the migraine that started ten minutes ago.

"Listen, I don't want you worrying about your shift and all. I cleared it with the captain and I'll cover your shift. I promise to keep you posted when the forensics come in or if they find Scott. Okay?"

I looked up, annoyed. Billings could see it in my eyes. "Come on, Billings," I pleaded. "You gotta convince the captain I can handle this. This is my brother, for Christ's sake. I need to stay in the loop."

He put his hand on my shoulder. "You know I will, John. You just cannot be *actively working* the case. You know that. There's a conflict of interest. I promise you that myself and Officer Putnam will tell you as much as we can, okay?"

I nodded and walked away to find Anna, once again. The crowd had dispersed and an officer was at the curb keeping the media at bay. He pointed towards the front door when I asked about Anna. Apparently, she was done giving her statement and went inside to rest.

I walked toward the couch, where she was laying down with her babies. I guess they can sense when she was distraught, since they were purring and licking her face and hands.

"How are you, sweetheart?"

"Oh, John, there you are! This whole thing is a nightmare! Who was that poor woman?" Anna asked.

I explained that the victim was Tess, Scott's Tess, and that I was off the case because of the conflict of interest. Understandably, Anna was in shock. We both were too scared and ashamed to ask the question that was lingering in the air. Could Scott have murdered Tess?

We were on the couch together theorizing about how she got there, what type of trouble Scott had gotten into, and if he was hiding out. Or what if something had happened to him too? I normally don't like to have these types of conversations with Anna, because I don't like to encourage her, but this case was different. It touched our lives, had happened in our home, and it involved family.

Theorizing seemed to work up an appetite, so Anna headed to the kitchen to heat up two plates. The spaghetti alla puttanesca had gone cold hours ago.

Just then, Anna's cell phone rang. I could hear the panicked voice from across the room. It was Shirlene. She must have learned about the murder from a news broadcast.

All I heard was Anna trying to calm her down. "Yes…uh huh…no, we're fine. That's not necessary...we don't know why she was there…no sign of him yet…okay…I'll talk to you later…I will…uh-huh, okay, bye-bye."

After Anna hung up, she recapped the call, and continued heating up our plates. We ate in silence with Jeopardy on in the background. I was eating slowly, dreading the call I had to make after I had taken my last bite. I had to call my parents and tell them what was going on. I assumed they hadn't seen the news yet, or they would have called already. Maybe they would have contact information for Tess's family. Somebody had to inform them before they saw it on the news.

Outside, I could hear the CSU techs and patrol cars heading out. I'm assuming Carmen was given isntructions NOT to give me those details I asked for, since no one had rang the bell. I'll get with Billings tomorrow after he meets with Doc Bernstein.

I was about to clean up the dishes when Anna took over. She apparently had the urge to bake. I've noticed Anna likes to bake when she's worried or stressed, maybe it's a way for her to channel her nervous energy. I left her in the kitchen with a recipe for cannolis with crushed pistachios on the counter. (See Appendix for recipe)

I grabbed my cell phone and went into the bedroom for privacy. I scrolled through my contacts, found my parent's number, and pressed the dial button. The phone was ringing.

Here goes nothing!

CHAPTER 11

A Shot of Tequila Before I Run

Scott

Well, I'm officially in hiding. When Tess told me she was having doubts about our relationship on the phone earlier this morning, I lost it. She was convinced I was shacking up with some broad, *even though I told her I was with my brother*, and swore she would find out the truth. By the time we hung up, I needed a drink bad. Calls and texts from my supervisor and sponsor kept coming, and I just couldn't face them. Now, I'm hiding from three people.

My phone vibrated again, and it was a text from John. "WHERE ARE YOU? CALL ME BACK!" All caps means I must be in trouble. Looks like he tried calling twice as well, based on the missed call icons on my screen. Oh well, I guess that makes four people I was hiding from.

Tess was the only bit of hope I had left in life, and I was not going to let her go without a fight, but for now, all I could think about was a drink. I was at the bar on my third shot of tequila, chatting up a cute blond when everyone at the bar starts staring at me funny. I thought to myself 'oh no, the paranoia is back', but then, I saw them moving their heads back and forth between me and the TV on the wall.

The bartender turned up the volume and that's when I saw it. The murder of a woman, at Anna's house, and the police want to question 'this man' regarding her death, who was a guest at the home. *MY FACE flashed on the screen!*

All I remember was throwing money on the counter and running as fast as I could out the door. Who was that woman and why was she dead in my room?

Now, I'm getting calls and texts from my brother and another strange number, probably the police. I have to clear my head first, I can't pick up. What would I say?

Of course, the ex-con is a dead ringer for the murder. If I were the police, I'd suspect me too!

What kind of sick joke were these guys playing? I told them I would have their money in thirty days. Just when I thought my life couldn't get any worse.

Since my insurance policy was safe for the time being, I decided to head to the nearest train station. Like John always said, 'running is what I do best'. I headed to the ticket counter and purchased my ticket to freedom … however temporary that freedom may be.

I had an hour to kill before my train left, so I headed to the lounge area where the local news was playing. Suddenly, a picture flashes on the screen of the murder victim from Anna and John's house. I remember that picture from our trip to the beach one weekend. The wind blowing through her hair, a few strands landing in her face, through a smile that radiated in the sunlight. I'm speechless. The victim is Tess. My Tess.

My knees buckled, my jaw dropped, and a lump formed in my throat. Once the grief had washed over me, anger surfaced. I clenched my fists and punched the wall next to me. They were going to pay for this. A life for a life.

There was no doubt in my mind that I would be the next murder victim, if I did not disappear for a bit and figure out how to clear my name.

I pulled my hoodie up over my head and spent the remaining time in the farthest corner of the station, hoping no one recognized me from the news.

CHAPTER 12

I Investigate, Therefore I Am

Anna

John was off to work and the media were still camped out front like they never left. I packed John pepperoni bread to go with some antipasto salad for lunch and sent him off with a forced smile.

I needed to finish my conversation with Shirlene, so I texted her to see if she could Skype. She immediately responded 'yes'.

I shooed the cats from my desk and set up my laptop. I was still in my daisy pjs and my hair was pulled up in a messy ponytail, but today, I just didn't care. A murder had occurred at my home and I needed to talk to my best friend.

With TatorTot and Tiny on my lap, I pressed the green call button. Shirlene popped up on the screen after two rings with a look of concern on her face. She was also still in her pjs with a red scarf on her head and a light touch of lip gloss, which is more than I had ventured to do.

"Morning. How are you holding up?" she asked.

I grabbed Tiny's paw as he tried to type on the keyboard. "Ugh, Tiny stop it! Sorry, Shirlene. I'm hanging in there."

"Is John there with you?"

"Nope. Duty calls. He's got open cases to work, even though he is off this one."

"You want me to come over and sit with you?"

"Nah, I'm okay, thanks. Just wanted to talk. For the life of me, I cannot figure out why Scott's girlfriend came here and why Scott is nowhere to be found. Did I tell you the neighbor said he saw some 'seedy characters' on our street before the murder?"

"Oh my gosh! No, you did not! I told you from the beginning it was a mistake letting that man stay in your home.

He's an ex-con, for goodness sake! And, whatever trouble he *was* into, seems to have followed him there." She paused, as if finding the right words, before continuing. "I hate to even say this aloud, but…um…you don't think he had anything to do with the murder, do you?"

"Shirlene, no! Of course not! I mean, he happens to be John's brother and I figured if John said it was safe for him to come here, then it was safe. He *is* a cop, Shirlene."

"True. I know John wouldn't intentially put you in harm's way. But, still…"

"Well, you are not the only one reeling from the decision to let him stay here. John's parents are devastated. They just kept apologizing on the phone last night."

"Yeah, they did kind of push him on you guys."

"Enough about murder. Tell me about this new man. Any updates?"

"He's so wonderful, Anna…and rich! I've never been swept off my feet like this. He's been spoiling me since we first met. I actually said 'yes' to his invitation to spend a week in St. Thomas with him. The cruise ship leaves in two days."

"Whoa! That's moving fast, isn't it? You just met two weeks ago. I mean, what do you really know about this guy?"

"I know enough. At least all of the important stuff. I'll be fine, Anna. Don't worry."

She was smiling from ear-to-ear and I didn't want to spoil her 'new relationship' glow, but I was seriously worried.

"Okay. Do me a favor and email me the trip information and your gentleman friend's name, okay?"

She agreed and we disconnected, still thinking about her mysterious man.

As I stood up to head to the kitchen and make another cup of coffee, I peeked out the front window. Reporters were still there and I know the neighbors, as well as the community HOA, were going to be complaining soon. It was one thing to write about murders and get caught up in murders 'elsewhere', but not *inside* their quiet community. That was a no-no.

I was sipping my coffee and wondering what other problems followed Scott to my home and if he was more dangerous than John let on, when my cell phone dinged. It was John.

John: No one is keeping me in the loop. I'm going nuts.

Me: I can imagine.

John: I did get Tess's full name. It's Tess Waters. Scott told me she was a teacher's assistant in Newark for special needs kids.

Me: Oh okay, good.

John: Anything you could find out would be nice. I'm being watched here.

Me: Are you asking me to meddle, dear?

John: No, just making conversation, honey. Working on missing teen case…may be home late, sorry.

Me: No problem. Talk to you later. XXXOOO

This was a first! John was *asking me* to investigate, rather than butt out. I cannot lie, I had been dying for something to investigate for months. The excitement of 'murder' was missing from my life; which sounds very disturbing, when I say it aloud. Ha!

I headed back to the laptop and began to type *Tess Waters* plus several key words I knew about her into the search engine. After scrolling a couple of pages of photos, I found her social media pages for Facebook and Instagram.

I started with the Facebook link. It seems she was very close to her mother and sister. The cover photo was a picture of Tess, most likely her mother, and her younger sister at the beach. I scrolled her feed some more, but her activity had been low the past few weeks. The next picture was her and her sister at some type of outdoor rock concert. I could tell they were sisters by their similar features, but Tess was definitely the oldest. Her sister's name was Brit, short for Brittany, perhaps. I clicked on her name and it took me to her Facebook page. I was right, Brit *was* short for Brittany. Since most people have notifications on their phones nowadays, I thought I would try sending her a direct message. John's parents had already notified Tess's mother, so the family knew about her death.

Hello Brittany, You don't know me, but I am a friend of the family. I wanted to tell you how sorry I am for your loss. I was wondering if you had time to speak with me if you're feeling up to it. – Anna Romano

Within seconds my lapop dinged.

Hi Anna, Thank you for the condolences, but I can't talk now because I'm on the phone with an Officer Billings. I'll try to call you later this evening.

Oh crap. Caught red-handed. I hope I didn't just get John in trouble.

I responded to her message with my cell number and the agreement to speak later.

Well, I might as well check my email while I'm here. The messages for my Dear Jesse column were piling up. Women needing help with cheating husbands, men needing help with wives who were the breadwinners and made more money than them, and a few first date questions. I'll have to answer a few of these later.

There was a message from my mother. I sighed, hesitated for a moment, and clicked on the email to open it:

Hello Anna,

Remember me? Your mother. You avoid my calls and barely answer my emails anymore. Especially since you started dating that detective. Imagine my surprise when I saw you on the news this morning. Something about a murdered woman in your home. What in heaven's name have you gotten yourself involved in now? Call me right away.

Mom

Oh dear. I'll have to call her later. I'm sure her concern is genuine, but she'll also take any opportunity she can to grill me on the 'm' word and when I'm going to give her grandchildren. I keep telling her she had seven, with Tiny being the youngest. She just laughs.

I spent the rest of the day watching the food and travel channels on the couch in my pjs and by mid-afternoon I was getting antsy. I texted John, asking him if he wanted me to drop off dinner for him, but he replied he just wanted his favorite latte and a snack. After bickering back and forth about my safety and murderers on the loose, he conceded, since it was still light out at five o'clock. We agreed to a 'date' at five and I headed to the bedroom to get dressed.

It felt good to get out of the house. After peeking out the window for 'shady characters', I headed out past the reporters at four thirty to grab John's latte and meet up at the station. I repeated 'No comment' over and over, but the questions kept coming. *"Did you know the murdered woman? What was she doing in your home? Did you know she was staying there? Has Detective Solace been pulled from the case because his brother is a suspect in the murder?"*

I was in my car and pulling off when I saw Mr. Craigly cruising down the sidewalk heading towards the park. I slowed to a stop and rolled down the passenger side window to say hello.

"Afternoon, Mr. Craigly!"

"Miss Romano. Everything okay?"

"Yes, I just wanted to thank you again for staying with me yesterday until John arrived. I have a few cannoli left over from last night. Here you go."

I handed him the zip lock bag through the window and he snatched it up.

"Pistachios, that's new. They catch that killer yet?"

"Uh, no. But, I'm sure they will soon."

"Yeah, we all do. Lot of disruption to the neighborhood. I'm headed to the park, I'll see ya."

He was rolling off before I could even say goodbye. What a lovely man. Geez.

I'm running a few minutes late, so I picked up speed towards the coffee shop.

CHAPTER 13

Clandestine Meetings about LOVE (minus the E)

John

Anna is up to her snooping again, except this time it's with my blessing. Billings called me earlier to tell me he was on the phone with Tess's sister when she sent a message to her on one of those social media sites. I tried to sound annoyed, but wondered what she had found out. I'll have to find out later, since Billings asked me to meet him at the park up the street. He must have an update for me and doesn't want the higher-ups to know he's 'sharing'.

I have to hurry. I'm interviewing a suspect in my missing teen case this afternoon. I grabbed my jacket and headed out. It was a beautiful, sunny day, so I decided to walk.

Billings was at a bench on the south side of the park. I headed his way and sat down beside him.

"We spoke to the folks at the halfway house Scott was staying at before he moved in with Tess, as well as Tess's sister. We haven't been able to interview the mother yet. She's pretty shaken up. And, there's no father in the picture. He passed away two years ago."

I nodded and then asked, "What did the people at the halfway house say? And, what about his financials?"

"Yep. I was just getting to that. Apparently when your brother lost his job and Tess started threatening to kick him out, he borrowed money from the wrong people and became their personal transport person for – *get this* –illegal organs, to pay off the debt. Can you believe it?"

"What the — !" My jaw dropped, and I caught myself being observed by a group of mothers with strollers. I smiled apologetically, and quickly straightened my face back to a casual state.

Billings continued, "I also did some digging and found out a few of the deposits to his account were being made by a company called Leading Organ Vitality Incorporated, also known as L-O-V, or love. Pretty strange, right?"

"I'll say. Have you made contact with the company yet?"

"No luck getting through to anyone yet. Putnam figures it might be a shell company for something else. We're still tracking Scott's final movements for the day of the murder and checking all of the bus and train stations, as well as airports. Don't worry, sir, we are going to do our best to bring him in safely."

I nodded and stood up to walk back to the station feeling discouraged. I wished I could get in on the investigation. I know Billings and Putnam are doing their best, but I hated feeling so helpless.

Where are you, Scott?

CHAPTER 14

An Order of Mocha Java Jolt...with 50,000 Volts

Anna

After feeding Mr. Craigly, I headed to the café, the Twenty Volts Cafe, for John's favorite latte, *the double mocha lightning java jolt special*. I purchased a bagel with lox and cream cheese as well, to help him soak up all that caffeine.

A young girl with a hot pink mohawk punched a few keys on the register and shouted my order into the mic in some kind of special code I could not decipher, and then she handed me a receipt with my order number on it.

I was getting napkins at the condiment stand when a tall woman in a suit smiled at me and said hello. I smiled back and said the same in kind. She was quite attractive and was what some like to call 'put together'. I always admired women like her. Their hair and makeup were flawless and their outfit looked like it was assembled by a runway fashion designer for *Vogue.* My dad would say she was 'nothing but trouble with her perfect pearly whites and legs that won't quit'.

"I see you like the mocha lightning java jolt too. It's my favorite," the woman said happily, as she grabbed sugar packets and other random items.

She seemed nice enough, so I opted to not blow her off and answer her politely, instead.

"No, it's my *boyfriend's* favorite, and it's actually a double. I prefer tea."

Mohawk girl called out my number and I headed to the counter. I grabbed the bag and coffee cup and walked out the café. Surprisingly, and a bit awkwardly, at the same time as model-suit lady.

I waved for her to go first and she proceeded to walk in the same direction as my car. Geez, just my luck!

"Well, my husband is waiting in the car, nice meeting you! Have a nice day!"

She was waving while I was nodding politely and looking for my keychain at the same time.

I was cursing to myself about the long walk to the side of the building with my order, because all the spaces in front of the cafe were full. I could hear John preaching to me in my head. Always have your keys out, be alert, pay attention to your surroundings, blah, blah, blah…

I was so distracted by my own thoughts, I didn't see the van pull up behind me. Two men in black jumped out. The mocha java jolt and bag of food fell to the ground along with my keys when I felt the hard steel object press into my back. I was directed to 'get in the van and no one would get hurt'. Why do criminals always say that right before they hurt you?

I remember wondering to myself what LOV stood for on the side of the van, when a volt of electricity knocked me off of my feet. I was being shoved into the back of the van.

CHAPTER 15

Can You Hear Me Now?

John

I had just released the suspect in the case of the missing teen, Joy Brannon. His alibi checked out, but he did provide some great information on the last person to see her before she went missing. I had finally narrowed the timeline down to within an hour.

I was about to run a search on this new lead when my desk phone rang. My nerves were shot and I was dying for a coffee.

"Solace!" I barked into the phone.

"Oh my, is that how you answer the phone at your place of work? That is not proper manners Johnny. I taught you much better than that. You know – "

I cut my mother off politely. "Of course not, Mom, I'm sorry about that. I'm on a big case that has me stressed. You usually call my cell. What's up?

"Well, your father and I want to know what's going on with your brother's case. Any word from Scott?" she asked.

"Nothing yet, but I'll keep you informed as soon as –"

"Hello! Can you hear me? Stupid cordless phone!" My father was trying to pick up another line in the house. I wonder when they set that up.

"Yes, we can hear you just fine! Stop yelling, Frank!" Esther scolded.

"Hi Dad, when did you get another line? Nevermind, anyway, I can hear you. What's up?"

"Your mother and I want to know what's going on with your brother's case."

I repeated the same thing I told my mother, while covering my face with my hands in frustration. I finally got them off the phone by telling them a teen kidnapper was 'literally' getting away as we speak and I had to go.

I love my parents dearly, but when they moved into the 'elderly' category they became a handful. I wonder if that will be me and Anna twenty years from now. I chuckled to myself.

By the way, where was Anna? It was almost six o'clock and she was supposed to be here by five. She texted me 45 mins ago that she was bringing me a mocha java jolt latte and a bagel with lox. Even with traffic it wouldn't take this long from up the street to get here. It's not like her to be late.

I called her cell, but it went straight to voicemail.

Something doesn't feel right.

I grabbed my keys and rushed for the front door in a whirlwind of emotions. I was scared that something had happened to Anna and that it was related to Scott's case, and felt guilty because we didn't insist a police detail be with her at all times.

I let the front desk know I was heading out for a break and to radio me with any emergencies.

Ten minutes later, I pulled up to the café, and spotted Anna's car in the side lot. There was something on the ground next to the driver's side door. I slowed down barely enough to put the car in park, jumped out, and went over to investigate.

It was a bag of food and a coffee cup. I knew better than to touch anything until I could get CSU out here. I turned and walked in the direction of my car to radio it in and grab a few flourescent cones, when I noticed something else. The back tires were flat. Actually, they appeared to be slashed.

Then I knew something was terribly wrong.

I jumped on the radio and reported the scene, and requested CSU assistance.

Next, I texted Billings and asked him to meet me at the Twenty Volts Café asap.

I have no doubt this has something to do with Scott's mess and I swear I will kill him if *anything* happens to Anna.

I pulled the yellow crime scene tape and cones out of my trunk and started securing the scene.

CHAPTER 16

Kidnappers with Manners

Anna

Ugh. Where am I? And, why do I feel like I've been run over by a truck?

My vision was slowly coming back into focus and for some reason I was freezing. I was on my back and my hands were tied behind my back.

I could tell I was in the back of some type of van or truck because of the swaying movement and sound of the motor. The windows on the back doors seemed to have been blacked out with something and I was surrounded by little red and white containers. They almost look the coolers you see in hospital shows where they have to rush the organ to a surgeon before the – I gulped. "Oh no, they couldn't be. All of them. Full of –." I was going to be sick. I tried to breathe deeply, but I was too cold. It was now apparent why the truck was so cold. It was refrigerated to keep the 'you know whats' alive or fresh, or something like that.

I started contemplating the last thing I could remember before I ended up here.

I remember placing my order at the café, grabbing my order, and walking to the car. But, I don't remember getting into the car. That's right! There was something stuck in my back and a man's voice, and then I dropped John's coffee and food.

What would anyone want with me? I can't imagine another crazed psycho read one of my books and thought I was talking about him, or her. Geez.

Another memory returned. Before I hit the ground from whatever incapicitated me, I saw the van. The letters LOV was on the side of the van with a logo of a red heart. It was the same logo on the side of all these little coolers. As a matter of fact, I recall the same logo on the badge of that model lady at the café. It was on a lanyard around her neck. Probably some type of security badge for her company.

I was looking around on the floor for my purse, but the kidnappers must have taken it. However, they did not search me, because if they did, they would have noticed the cell phone in my jacket pocket. Ha! Jokes on you!

I had to get free and call for help…somehow.

Just then, I lunged sideways as the van came to a sudden halt. As I peeked through the cracks in the black covering of the back windows, I could see it was even darker than before.

The back doors were thrown open by a broad, muscular man in a white polo shirt and jeans with the same heart logo and LOV lettering on the shirt. He smiled casually and announced, "Final stop! Everybody out!"

My eyes were adjusting to the light and I was attempting to stand when she appeared. It was the lady in the suit from the café. But why? What did she have to do with this?

The muscular guy helped me jump down from the back of the van. I made sure to keep my arm close to my side pocket so that the phone stayed in place and hidden.

I wanted to wipe that smirk off of her perfect 'put together' face. And, I was about to tell her so, when a tall, distinguished gentlemen in an expensive navy suit and blinding gold and diamond cuff links came from the side of the van and joined her.

They both reeked of money and power and wore the same pompous smirk on their faces.

The woman finally greeted me, and as if we were old friends. "Anna," she gushed, "so lovely to see you again, dear. I hope the ride wasn't too uncomfortable for you. Welcome to

LOV, pronounced just like the term of endearment and romance. Love. I am Vanessa and this my husband, Oscar."

Her heels clicked on the concrete of the underground garage, as she walked ahead of me, turning back slightly to speak. Her arm gestures were grand, in contrast with her husband's quiet demeanor. She continued her spiel, "Come! Let me show where you will be staying… temporarily."

"Why are you doing this? Does this have something to do with Scott? I really don't want to be in the middle of things. I just want to go home," I implored.

"Yes dear, we know exactly what's waiting back home for you. Besides those awful creatures you like to call your 'babies', there is a handsome detective, or what we like to call 'leverage'." There was that pompous smirk again.

I was so stunned I couldn't even respond. Although unclear about how she knew so much about me, one thing was for certain – I was the pawn in their sick little game and Scott was the center of it somehow.

As if reading my mind, the woman now known as Vanessa continued her story. "You see, dear woman, you are simply a pawn in our plan to get Scott to 'cooperate' and repay the money owed to us. And, since he seems to be, um, what's the word, darling?" She looked to her husband for clarity, crinkling her forehead and snapping her fingers in the air.

"M. I. A.," her husband grumbled.

"Yes, that's it, that's the term. So, as I was saying, since Scott is M. I. A., the cop brother's girlfriend will do just fine as an incentive for Scott to do the right thing."

Speaking for a second time since our meeting, her husband muttered, "I still say we should have snatched up the cop brother."

"That would have been too dangerous, darling. We talked about this already and I decided I wanted the author-cat lady," she announced firmly.

I heard a low 'Yes, dear' from the husband and the subject was dropped. I can see who wears the Armani suit in this family.

We reached a pair of double glass doors and stepped inside a small lobby with a set of elevators. There was a sign that read LOV Inc. – 5th Floor. The up arrow lit up and we stepped inside. The muscular guy in the white polo inserted a special key into the panel and pressed the unluckiest number – *thirteen*. That's when I knew I was doomed.

The elevator dinged and the doors opened at the thirteenth floor. It seemed to be an unoccupied floor where construction was taking place, because there were no employees or furniture anywhere. They apologized for the mess and told me to watch my step as I stepped over tools, plywood, paint cans, and other construction items. They had to be the most polite kidnappers ever, except for the tasing part. Ha!

They led me to a room in the back of the office space. It was the only enclosed room, as far as I can see. There was glass across the front, but the rest of the walls were solid and soundproofed with heavy padding, like the black foam they use in recording studios. A single window was visible in the back of the room.

"Well, this is your spot, dear. Make yourself comfortable. Bruno will be right outside if you need anything at all," Vanessa explained.

The muscle man now had a name. Bruno waved shyly at me when his name was mentioned. I smiled back awkwardly. These people were beyond bizarre.

Bruno pulled out a pocket knife, turned me around, and cut the zip tie that bound my hands. I thanked him and rubbed my wrists noting the rash that had formed. Bruno turned and left, locking the door behind him.

I found the furthest corner of the room and slid down to the floor. Somehow I had found myself in yet another dangerous situation. Even though these kidnappers were nicer than Frederick Talon, I'd rather be home with my babies.

But, I have faith John will find me in time. Or, at least find Scott, and get him to give them what they want, so they'll let me go.

Bruno was at the front of the office, in deep conversation with the Armani couple, the owners of LOV Inc. I tried to look natural as I reached into my pocket with one hand and attempted to text John with one hand. Thank goodness I never upgraded my phone to the latest technology, which was much larger, otherwise I think they would have found it on me. Yep, I still loved my small, handy flip phone.

I clicked the envelope icon for messaging and tapped John's name. Almost there. Now to send a message John would figure out. I was on the third letter, when there was a loud voice from the front of the office.

"Check her again!" Vanessa yelled.

They must have realized my purse did not have a phone in it.

Bruno was rushing towards me. I texted another two letters and hit Send and then the Home button, hoping he would not know how to view the latest activity on the phone.

He unlocked the door and burst in yelling, "Where is it, lady?"

"Where's what?" I replied, acting confused.

He forced me to stand up and patted me down, ultimately finding the flip phone in my jacket pocket.

Bruno shouted to his boss that he had located the phone. As he left the room, he turned to announce he would be back with my dinner shortly, as if nothing ever happened.

I half-smiled and nodded in confusion, while hoping to myself John would be able to decipher my rushed, cryptic message.

CHAPTER 17

A Visit from the Gentlemen in Black Suits

John

Victor from CSU was out front processing Anna's car and the surrounding area, and I was interviewing the café staff with Billings. Apparently she was talking to a woman they didn't recognize as a regular, and they walked out together.

"Any chance those surveillance cameras up there are working?" I said to the young girl with the pink mohawk as I pointed towards the ceiling by the front door of the café.

"Sorry, those are just for show. The boss thinks they keep us from getting robbed at night."

"Okay, thanks anyway."

She graciously replenished our caffeine levels and sent us on our way.

"What now, sir?" Billings asked.

I was about to respond, but my phone vibrated. I checked the screen and immediately shouted, "It's Anna!"

"Oh wow! Is she okay?" Billings inquired anxiously.

"I'm not sure. The message says: lov got m."

"Love like l-o-v-e?"

"What does it matter how she spelled it?"

"Can I take a look, sir?"

I handed the phone to Billings.

His face dropped. "You remember that organ donor company I told you about? What if she was trying to say 'LOV got me'? You know, like they were the ones who grabbed her!"

I nodded in agreement and asked if he received any information on their corporate headquarters.

At that moment, Billings's radio squawked. It was the captain. He said he needs to see both of us in his office *pronto*!

As much as I wanted to follow up on this lead to find Anna, I could not afford to blow off the captain and lose any connection to Scott's case. I just know it's the key to finding Anna.

As we sprinted to our cars, I called out to Victor to page me if he found anything. He yelled back some type of response with 'dude' in it and gave me a thumbs-up. I just shook my head and started the car. Victor was working solo, so I guess Doc Bernstein and Carmen were out on other calls.

Billings and I met up ten minutes later at the precinct. The captain's office was known as the fishbowl, because of the wall of glass that went all the way around the front. You could see everything going on, unless somebody was being chewed out, then the mini-blinds were drawn tight. But today, they were open, and there seemed to be a couple of suits in there already with the captain. The first thing that came to mind was the Feds. He saw us through the glass and gestured for us to come in.

After the captain introduced them as *gentlemen from the FBI* who were 'interested' in our case involving LOV Inc., I couldn't help but think it was good sign that the captain was even letting me in on this meeting. Billings and I sat while the suits spoke.

The older, gray-haired man with the distinguished face and serious expression spoke first.

"We've been following LOV for four months now and invested a lot of man hours in building a case against the company for acquiring and selling illegal body parts. Believe it or not, there is a billion-dollar black market for wanted organs. And, we are just about ready to make a move to execute search warrants and shut them down once and for all."

His partner nodded in agreement with the same stern expression.

The captain interjected. "So, what is it you need from us?"

"We need you to fall back," said the older FBI agent.

"No way, this is our case!" I was boiling hot with rage and began to stand up, but Billings quickly pressed his hand on my shoulder to sit back down.

The captain intervened. "Listen, we want to help in any way that we can, but this case is very personal to the precinct. It involves the brother of one of our own. Detective Solace's brother," he pointed. "Surely, you can understand?"

"And, now, we think they may have kidnapped his girlfriend, Anna!" Billings chimed in.

"I see. We were not aware of this," the agent responded with a look of concern.

"So, you see, sir, we have a vested interest in this case and want to get Scott and Anna back safely," the captain countered.

"The FBI has no interest in Anna, but there is evidence that this Scott was somehow involved in transports for LOV, and we *will* take him down if need be. Just so that we are clear."

The captain must have noticed my face getting redder by the minute and jumped in before I could respond.

"How about this? We will agree to work 'together' on the case, as long as you vow to help us get Anna back safely and share any information you gather on the case *before* you move in with arrests."

The FBI finally agreed to our terms, but I'm not too sure how much their 'word' meant based on previous experience. They told us they already had a list of properties for LOV to narrow down their main location where the two owners are hiding out, so they can initiate their sting operation. They just needed our help with one thing… bringing Scott in.

Something was fishy about this whole setup with the FBI, but I couldn't put my finger on it. I was just glad the captain was letting me stay in the loop, even though I was not *officially* on the case.

I was glad, however, that Billings and Putnam were on the case. They know Anna personally and I knew they would do everything humanly possible to bring her home safely.

Billings was still a bit starry-eyed over Putnam, but focused all the same. Putnam made grade last month and we all went out to celebrate her new rank. Everyone was out of uniform, hanging out at a local restaurant. We had reserved a table of ten for her closest friends from the precinct, including myself and Billings. She walked in all smiles in a denim dress that hugged her suprisingly curvy, hourglass shape, and a pair of brown cowboy boots. Her hair was down and flowing past her shoulders and her dark olive skin was glowing, even in the dim light of the bar. Billings and I were floored, since we had never seen her out of uniform. She'd been to the house for dinner with Anna, me, and Billings of course, but always in uniform, since she was on call.

That was when Billings became even more starry-eyed. They started dating a few weeks after that.

So now the ball was in their court.

The fates of my brother, Scott, and my love, Anna, were in their hands.

I trust them completely. But…

CHAPTER 18

A Turkey Club and the Search for the Book

Anna

I really hope John understood my partially finished cry for help. Earlier, Muscle Man brought me a turkey club, chips, and a bottled water, plus he let me use the restroom. He even asked me if I needed a blanket, since there wasn't any vents in here and the temperature dropped at night.

I decided to take him up on the offer and hunkered down in the corner for what was sure to be a very long night. Maybe Muscle Man would fall asleep and I could get away. Although, I would have to get out of this locked room first and picking locks is not really a skill of mine.

There were loud voices coming from the front of the office again. I crawled towards the door, careful to remain below the glass windows, and attempted to hear what they were saying. I could only make out bits and pieces, but I definitely heard Scott's name. And they kept referring to a book. What kind of book? It would have to a very important book for them to be arguing over it. I'm pretty sure they're not talking about one of mine.

Scott better hope John and Billings can find him before these people, because they sound pretty angry.

I crawled back to my corner near the window and stood up to look out. There were a sea of cars interspersed with people coming and going as if all was right with the world. Some of the them were carrying coffee cups, some carrying briefcases, and many of them in business suits nodding and smiling at each other as they fanned in and out of the building. They have no idea what this company is really into, and frankly, neither do I.

If I screamed at the top of my lungs right now, no one would hear me way up here on the non-existent 13th floor. I was thinking of throwing something heavy against the window, but I was sure it was shatterproof and soundproof. And, besides, what would I use, my empty water bottle? It's not like when I was on the boat with Frederick Talon and found that fire extinguisher. That would definitely make a dent in the window. I cringed at the memory of having to clobber Talon on the head right before the boat exploded. Ahhhh, fun times.

I was so caught up in my 'flashback', I didn't hear suit lady approach. Bruno had let her in, but remained outside the door.

She was so smiling and friendly as she approached me, I was expecting her to ask me if I was 'enjoying my stay'.

"Tell me what you know about Scott," she asked pointedly.

"Not much. I know that he's John's brother, had a troubled life, did some jail time for fraud, I think."

She clenched her fists angrily. "No, no, I mean, what do you know about Scott and his 'business' with us, with LOV?!"

This is the first time she had raised her voice towards me and I was a bit stunned. It seems the princess has a dark side.

"Nothing, I swear. I don't know anything."

"I don't believe you. I think you are holding back information to protect your precious cop boyfriend."

"That's all John told me! I'm telling the truth!"

"Enough! I have some business to take care of, but when I return we will discuss this matter again. And, next time, I won't ask so nicely."

She yelled for Bruno to lock up my area and keep a close eye on me, and then clicked off hastily in her red-bottomed shoes.

I spent the rest of the evening looking out of the window and watching the sun go down.

As darkness fell, I thought of my babies and wondered if John had gone home to feed them yet.

A Trip to PA Hits a Harsh Detour

John

With Anna on my mind, I was barely able to finish an arrest report and was comtemplating heading home when Billings called my cell.

"We got him, sir."

"Scott? That's great, where did you find him? Is he okay?"

"Yeah, he's fine. We got a tip from a clerk at the bus station who remembers selling him a ticket to Reading, PA."

"Well, that's one place to 'blend in' and hide out for a while."

"Yeah, that was exactly his intention, too. We tracked the bus to a rest stop in PA and picked him up. We're heading back to the precinct now. We're about 45 minutes away."

I disconnected the call and a ton of questions I wanted to ask Scott began to flood my mind. Before I got carried away, I texted my parents to let them know we found Scott, that he was okay, and I'd call them later.

I busied myself with more paperwork for the next 45 minutes until Billings and Putnam walked through the front door of the precinct with my brother in handcuffs between them. I wish I could say this was the first time I had seen my brother in cuffs, but it wasn't. However, it still caused angst in my chest and a lump in my throat when I tried to speak, as if I was about to choke on tears. I collected myself, stood up, and charged towards them. As I did so, I realized I was losing my cool, and all of the worry, fear, frustration, and anger of the past two days took control of my body.

I grabbed Scott by the front of jacket and shook him as hard as I could. "How could you? What did you do? I swear if anything happens to Anna, I'll kill you!"

Billings and Putnam were just as caught off guard as I was. Probably because they had never seen me so angry.

It only took them a few seconds to break Scott free of my grip and calm me down, but not before the captain ran out of his office to catch the ending.

"Get him into Interrogation Room 4! Solace, my office, NOW!" the captain commanded.

I hustled into the office behind the captain and began to apologize.

"I'm sorry, sir, I lost my tem- "

"Save it, Solace! You know, I have been nothing but understanding and fair with this whole case. Letting you in on information about your brother, even though I shouldn't have."

I held my head down humbly while nodding in agreement.

"I'm willing to let you OBSERVE the interview, but you gotta promise me you can keep it together."

"I promise, sir. I lost my cool. It won't happen again."

"You're damn right it won't! Now, let's go. I haven't let the Feds in on our capture…yet. I want us to have first dibbs on the interview and see what we can find out."

We hurried over to Interrogation Room 4, and I watched my brother with Putnam from behind the glass. Scott was sitting down and handcuffed to the front of the gray metal table. The captain flipped the switch for the audio and we listened in.

Putnam was sitting across from Scott, listening intently and nodding her head. Her expression was warm and caring.

"Like I said before, I'm sorry about Anna, but I'm positive they are not going to hurt her because they need me alive!"

"What makes you say that?" Putnam asked.

"Because, they just won't, okay? That's all I can say or they'll kill me! They already took Tess from me! Don't you see?!" Scott screamed hysterically.

I had never seen my brother so scared.

Just then, Billings stormed into the room. The door slammed against the wall with a loud bang that startled everyone, including me. He asked Putnam for some 'time alone' with the suspect and Putnam shook her head and turned to Scott. "You should have talked to me while you had the chance, Scott."

It was the classic 'good cop, bad cop' routine. Billings and I had done it a million times. But this time, Billings's anger was real. He was just as worried about Anna as I was.

He got 'up close and personal' with Scott – close enough to make Scott uncomfortable and lean back in his chair.

Billings remained standing and towered over him, before he bent down to look him square in the eyes.

"I have a very personal interest in this case, Scott. And, do you wanna know why this case is so important to me?" Billings's low but harsh tone of voice was getting to Scott. He was so close they were almost touching noses.

When Scott did not answer, he slammed his fist on the table, and barked, "Do ya?!"

Scott nodded his head up and down with widening eyes.

Billings continued, "Because John is my partner. And partners look after each other. If someone messes with him or someone he loves, I take that personally."

He sat down in the chair next to Scott and pulled it closer to his chair, almost touching his leg.

"So, here's what you're gonna do. You're gonna start talking, you spineless piece of crap, at least for your brother's sake, and you're gonna tell us everything from the very beginning, when you first got involved with LOV. Am I making myself clear?"

Scott nodded and broke down. "Okay, okay, but I swear I didn't know what this company was into. It was only supposed to be for a few months to pay off my gambling debt."

Scott explained it all started at the racetrack with a bet on a 'sure thing', but swears he only did it to win money for the household, to help Tess with the bills. He got in over his head with a bookie named Luke and it went downhill from there. Luke told him that the only way to pay him back the money was to perform some favors for him, transporting organs to different hospitals and universities. But he came to find out, it wasn't Luke that ran the bookie operation, but LOV Inc.

Scott thought the company was legit, but then found out they handle illegal organ extractions and donations on the side. He started getting suspicious when the pickups were at various storage units in the middle of the night, and later found out some of the donors were paid for their organ donation, but many were not.

He started snooping and keeping a log of the locations and deliveries. It turns out LOV was snatching prostitutes and homeless people from the streets, people that no one would miss, and extracting their organs. Oftentimes, leaving them for dead.

During a visit to one of the corporate offices, he came across an official book with entries of all the illegal donors, the money received for the organs, the extractor names, and the extraction location. The locations matched up with his personal log. Based on the names of some of the extractors, a lot of medical professionals would be ruined, along with the hospitals they were affiliated with.

Now, LOV wants their book back, plus the balance of the money he owes them for his gambling debt, and, oh yeah, his life.

As I listened to my pathetic brother tell his story, I was thinking to myself that even if they got the book back, that doesn't mean they won't kill him and Anna. These people have nothing to lose.

Billings waited for a pause in his story and interjected. "Where was the office where you found the book, Scott?"

Before Scott could answer, loud voices could be heard in the hallway outside the door.

"Where is he?! You have five seconds to tell us where he is!"

Uh-oh, the jig is up. I knew the loud booming voice of the FBI anywhere. Once the Feds get this case, we have zero chance of getting Anna home safely. Their number one priority would be shutting down LOV.

The gentlemen in suits busted into Interrogation Room 4. Putnam rushed in behind them with her hands up apologizing to Billings for not being able to stall them longer.

"This interview is OVER! We only agreed to this arrangement if you came clean on everything you uncovered. Now we're taking over OFFICIALLY."

Billings unlocked the handcuffs and handed Scott over to them, while Scott yelled and pleaded for someone to help him.

I remember Scott looking into the one-way mirror calling my name, and asking me to help him. That lump in my throat returned and I felt so helpless and unable to assuage his fears. What was I going to tell my parents now? That I had him here, safe, and then I lost him?

We were officially out of the loop.

Billings tried to calm Scott down, promising him we would straighten it all out and get him back into our custody soon.

Now at another dead end, I begrudgingly called my parents with an update before heading home to tend to the babies.

As the sun went down, I tried not to think about what my Anna could be going through at this very moment.

The Balcony Escape to the Gym

Scott

As soon as we pulled up, I could tell it was a dump. From the tattered sign that sadly advertised the OTL had a CANCY for just $29.99, to the faded, yellowish stucco that probably used to be white back in the day. There was a liquor store across the street and an all-night diner next door, which I guess is the only reason this place is still open, along the with cheap rates, of course.

I asked the agents why we were here, but they just gave me the same shtick as earlier, that it was for my own safety, blah blah blah. The only reason I was being protected is because I agreed to help them build their case against LOV Inc.

There was no check-in, so I assumed this was a place the Feds used frequently. They pulled around the back and into the space for Room 22. There were a few homeless people rummaging through the trash bins behind the diner a few yards away, but other than that, it was fairly quiet.

The room was on the second floor and had the usual motel ambiance and disinfectant smell. Two double beds, one bathroom, one closet, one dresser, one small TV, one table, and two chairs.

They directed me to the chair next to the table and hooked up my bracelets to the chair while they checked the room. For what, I don't know.

A few minutes later, there was a knock at the door. Another agent appeared in the doorway, and said something about checking in for the night shift. Apparently, he would be guarding the door outside. Great! There goes my first escape plan. I have to get out of here and try to save Anna. I bring so much drama to everyone's lives. She's a nice lady and my brother is lucky to have her. I don't want to be the one to ruin his happiness.

I continued my own scan of the room when my eyes landed on the curtains that went all the way down to the floor. That's when I realized it was not covering a window, but a sliding glass door leading to a balcony! That's going to be my ticket out of here. I just have to finagle my way out of these handcuffs.

One of the agents announced he was going next door to pick up some food. That leaves me with just one elderly guy. I'm pretty sure I can outsmart him, if I plan it right.

"Excuse me, sir," I asked politely. "Would it be okay if I used the john? It's been a long drive, if you know what I mean."

"Okay, but no funny business. I'm going to uncuff you, but just remember there is another agent right outside that door," he pointed. "Understood?"

"Yeah, sure, no funny business. I promise."

He uncuffed me and ushered me into the bathroom. Once inside, I looked around desperately for a weapon of sorts while pretending to 'use the bathroom' with flushing sounds and running water. I found what I needed on the toilet. The lid to the tank. It was heavy and I don't want to kill the guy, just render him incapacitated for a minute, while I get to those sliding doors behind the curtains.

I opened the door just a crack to see where he was, but there was no one in the room. Then, I noticed the door to the room was slightly ajar. He must have been talking to the goon out front. I placed the toilet lid down on the sink and quietly creeped over to the curtains and slid the door open. Next, I stepped out on the balcony and gauged the distance I would have to jump, when I saw the fire escape ladder. This night just keeps getting better and better.

I was on the third rung when a shout came from above. "Hey, get back here!"

There was more yelling to cut me off at the lower level and not let me get away. I descended the ladder at lightening speed and took off for the street that ran behind the motel where there was less lighting.

Ignoring the loud voices behind me, I just kept running. I was finally able to find a cab and hitch a ride to the 24-hour gym where I hid the book. John got me a guest membership on his family plan when I first got here, although I've never seen him come in and work out once.

The FBI thinks the flash drive I gave them with pictures of each page was all I had, but it wasn't. I have the hard copy of the book hidden in my locker.

It was a little after three in the morning when we pulled up to the front doors of the gym. There was no one at the front desk and only a few guys over at the bench press making grunting sounds. I dipped into the locker room, opened the locker, and retrieved the book and some cash I had stored there for protein bars and smoothies from the gyms's juice bar. Now, I just have to get to the LOV building in Hamilton. It was where I stole the book and I'm positive it's where they are holding Anna. The owners, Vanessa and Oscar Santiago, have their offices on the fifth floor.

I asked the cab to wait for me out front, so I hopped in and gave him the address to the LOV building.

I arrived at LOV's Hamilton offices without a weapon or a plan. I just knew I had to make things right with John and get Anna out of my mess. The book was tucked in my waistband and I was hoping it would be enough for the psycho power couple to let her go. I knew they were up there because this was one of the nights I usually dropped off deposits with Luke.

I paid the cab fare and the driver took off in a flash, not wanted to bear witness to what was about to happen with me and a closed, dark building.

I stepped quickly around to the side service entry door. The keypad was next to the metal door and I was hoping the code had not changed since I was last here. 2 – 7 – 3 – 7 – 4 - * …the door beeped and a green light glowed with its approval for me to enter. Thank goodness! Now to get up to the 5th floor inconspicuously. I decided to take the stairs.

Two steps at a time, I ascended, until I reached the fifth floor door. I opened it slowly to see if the guard was around. Suddenly, I was greeted by a pair of eyes and a coy smile.

"Scott, we've been waiting for you. Come in, please," Oscar Santiago insisted, while grabbing me by my collar.

"Ow! Easy Oscar! How did you know I was here?"

"You of all people should know we have eyes all over the property."

"Please don't hurt me. I have what you want!" I begged.

"That's for my wife to decide. Let's go!" Oscar yelled, while continuing to drag me down the hallway to their offices in the long, private corridor.

Vanessa was standing at her desk as we turned the corner. Her goon was nowhere in sight. She was wearing a skintight navy pants suit with a low cut blouse and and white strappy heels so pointy they could double as a weapon. Even at four in the morning, this woman could look like she was well-rested and ready to rule the world.

"You're looking well, Vanessa," I said slyly with a slight smile.

"Hey! That's Mrs. Santiago to you, buddy!" Oscar shouted.

I chuckled and shrugged. If only he knew the half of what Mrs. Santiago did after hours.

"Enough! We've been looking all over for you, Scott." She approached me slowly and a tad seductively, though her words were anything but seductive. "You've been a bad boy, Scott. You took something that did not belong to you. And, I'm sure you know what we do to people who betray us. Just ask your friend, Luke."

I was startled by her statement and asked what happened to him.

"We can call him if you like, darling." She snapped her fingers at her husband. "Oscar, get me the number to the County Morgue," she ordered, while laughing devilishly.

"Oh my God, Luke's dead too! But why? I had what you wanted! He had nothing to do with it!" I shouted.

"Oh, but darling, he had everything to do with it. He was the one who introduced you to our little side business, therefore, he was responsible for our…what do the courts call that, dear?" she snapped again at her husband.

"Pain and sufferin'" he replied.

"Yes, yes, pain and suffering. Thank you, love."

I rubbed my forehead in distress, choosing my words wisely before I spoke.

"I have what you want. The book is right here," I said, while holding the book in the air. "No one else has to get hurt and you can let Anna go."

"How can we be sure no copies were made?" Vanessa asked. She was standing with her arms crossed, head tilted and eyes squinted. "You've already proven yourself unworthy of our trust."

"How could I have made copies? I've been in custody all day; and, when I escaped, I went straight for the spot where I hid the book and came here!"

After careful consideration, they nodded to each other as if in mental agreement. Vanessa stepped towards me to take the book out of my hand, but I pulled back at the last second and stepped away from Oscar.

"Not quite. What about Anna?"

"I tell you what. You give us the book and make one final delivery for us, and we agree to wipe your debt clean and free your friend. Deal?"

I contemplated their offer. Deep down I knew it was a set up, and that I would ultimately end up like Luke. I made the decision to do whatever was necessary to ensure no one else got hurt. My life meant nothing without Tess anyway.

"Deal. Now, let me see Anna."

They led me to the elevator and we proceeded to the clandestine thirteenth floor. As we got off the elevator, I looked around at all of the construction equipment, scanning the room for Anna. They pointed at the glass room in the back of the office space. It was protected by Vanessa's goon. I stepped closer and saw Anna crouched in the corner with a blanket, fast asleep.

Vanessa gestured for the goon to grab me and hand her the book, so we can talk about the details of my final delivery.

We were standing by the elevators going over the pickup and delivery times, the package, and location. Oscar headed back down to the fifth floor, and Vanessa was scrolling on her phone trying to find an address. The goon was there, but leaning on a desk, and not paying too much attention. I noticed he was carrying a gun. It was tucked into a shoulder holster on his left side. I had to take my shot, so to speak. If I could just incapacitate him, I could restrain Vanessa and get Anna out of here.

Time to make my move! I step towards the goon, grab the gun from his holster, and take a shot at him, but, not before he knocks the arm holding the gun, causing me to miss his thigh. We were now in a wrestling match for the weapon. I could hear the elevator doors open and Oscar yelling something in Spanish.

At that very moment, before I could even get off another shot, an FBI team bursts through the stairway exit doors, while another team broke through the glass on the opposite side of the room.

An array of gunfire rang throughout the enclosed space and the goon grabbed the gun as I fell to the floor. My chest was on fire and the smell of smoke was in the air. Suddenly, I knew it was all over. Thoughts of my parents, my brother, and Tess in various moments in time, smiling, laughing, and crying, filled my head.

Instead of leaving behind a legacy, I had left behind a long line of turmoil and destruction for my loved ones to clean up.

CHAPTER 21

Shots Fired, Bullets Sprayed

Anna

I was on the floor resting under the blanket my captors gave me, when I heard the loud voices and a deafening boom soon after. I was sure it was a gun shot.

I stood up and immediately noticed Scott struggling with the guard for the gun. I yelled, "Scott, nooooo!!!" Our eyes met for an instant and I could have sworn he nodded at me, but I had no idea what it meant. Was it some sort of signal?

Just then, a whole row of windows to the left of where I was laying were shattered. Glass shards were flying everywhere and I dropped to the ground with the blanket over my head. The FBI flew through the windows on some type of harness and began exchanging gunfire with the guard and the Santiagos.

I crouched for as long as I could, hoping to avoid being hit by the spray of bullets flying back and forth across the office.

When all was quiet, I poked my head out from under the blanket to see if the coast was clear.

I was startled by a voice above me. "Ma'am, are you okay?" the large man with the SWOT vest asked.

"Yes, thank you."

He helped me stand and asked if I was Anna Romano.

I nodded my head, unable to speak from the shock of what had just occurred.

Minutes later, I remember him guiding me across the floor and the sound of glass crunching under our feet.

I also remember the sound of sirens in the distance, the sight of blood, and unidentifiable bodies on the floor.

I could not believe I had survived.

I wondered about my babies, if they were okay; but, I also wondered if John would be waiting for me outside, so that I could tell him how much I truly love him.

CHAPTER 22

I've Got a SWOT Story to Tell the World

John

I finally ended up going home after my shift. I made sure the cats were tended to and slipped into bed for a couple of hours' sleep.

An hour into REM my cell phone rang. It was Billings. I looked at the clock display and saw it was only 4am.

"Solace," I mumbled sleepily into the phone.

"Sorry to wake you, sir, but I thought you'd wanna know your brother escaped FBI custody."

I sit up in the bed wiping my eyes, unable to ascertain if I was dreaming or not.

"Sir, are you there?" Billings asked.

"Yeah, I was just catching a few hours sleep. I heard you. Do they know where he was heading?"

"I don't know, sir, but I may have an idea. I got a lead from an informant of mine and have the address of a building in Hamilton where the LOV associates may be holed up."

"That's great, Billings!"

"Thought you'd want to ride along, sir. Putnam and I can pick you up in, say, thirty minutes?"

"I'll be waiting out front," I answered. "Oh, and Billings?"

"Yeah?"

"Thanks."

"No problem, sir. You would do the same for me. See you in thirty."

I rushed to the bathroom for a quick shower and then suited up. I wasn't sure what we were walking into and I wanted to be prepared for the worst.

It was five in the morning when we made it to Hamilton. The sign said LOV offices were on the 5th floor and opened at seven. There was a second sign that said garage parking, but the gate was down. Was that where Anna was being held?

Since the doors were locked, our only choice is to sit tight down the street and keep a look out. We were no more than thirty minutes into our surveillance when a fleet of SWOT vans and unmarked cars (most likely, FBI) fly past us. We ducked down in our seats, so we wouldn't be noticed. If the FBI thought we were stepping on their case again, they would surely make us leave.

They positioned themselves by the front and back entrances, and had harnessed agents dropping from the roof, ready to swoop in through the windows. We could not figure out why they were so far above the fifth floor. What did they know that we didn't?

It was six am and the sun was rising, when they were all in position. Billings pulled the car closer to the back of the lot behind a brush of trees. There was a still calm in the air, yet I could feel my pulse racing.

However, once the movement began, it was as if I was watching it in slow motion. One team stormed in the front, while the other team stormed through the windows of what looked like the tenth or eleventh floor.

There was screaming and gunfire for what seemed to be minutes, but was probably less than sixty seconds. When the quiet still returned, I let out a sigh, not even realizing I had been holding my breath.

Billings pulled the car as close as he could to the front of the building and we all jumped out at once. The FBI agents put their hands out immediately to stop us from going any further.

"Whoa, whoa, who the hell are you? You can't go in there!" the large man with the gray hair and FBI vest rebuked.

He obviously did not remember us from the precinct, when he whisked my brother away in the middle of our interrogation.

We all flashed our badges and asked all at once what was going on, but we were shut down mid-flash. They didn't care who we were. This was an ongoing investigation and we were to wait *outside* the perimeter.

And, so, we waited. The media, ambulances, and eventually, the coroner's office started to arrive. The media stood behind us chattering about what they heard on the police scanners, and the medical personnel were guided through the front door in silence. I was unable to catch Doc Bernstein's attention.

A few big, bulky dudes came out first. They were in handcuffs. I'm guessing they worked security for LOV, based on the heart icon on their black t-shirts.

Next, a few random people, maybe the nightime cleaning crew, were guided out and taken aside for questioning.

Soon, a man and woman in expensive suits, covered in soot and debris, with their heads down were escorted out in handcuffs. Behind us, the media were in a frenzy trying to get a close-up of the pair and throwing questions at them like daggers. I assumed these were the owners of LOV, the people who kidnapped my Anna.

"Mr.and Mrs. Santiago! ...How are you going to plea to these charges? ...How many people died by your doctors' incompetence? ...Where did the organs go? ...Did you sell them?...Did you kidnap Anna Romano?"

The cameras flashed and the videos rolled while each station worked to improve their viewer ratings by providing a road to fame for the latest black market criminals.

At that very moment, my hope was restored, as I saw Anna appear in the doorway. She seemed dazed and confused, with small cuts on her face and arms, but still beautiful to me.

When she made eye contact with me she broke free from the agent who was escorting her and ran towards me. I met her with open arms and hugged her tightly.

"I thought I'd never see you again," she said to me as she cried softly in my arms.

"Me too, my precious rosebud. Me too."

"I love you, John."

I told Anna I loved her more than life itself and just then, Billings and Putnam walked up and asked Anna if she was okay. They wanted to get her over to the medic to have her cuts treated.

We were just about to turn and head over to the ambulance when the FBI stopped us.

"Which one of you is related to Scott Solace?"

Anna looked as if she knew what they were going to say.

"I am. Detective John Solace."

* * *

The agent pulled me aside, put his hand on my shoulder with his head bent down towards mine, in a serious stance. He told me that Scott was in the way of the gunfire and lost his life. He was shot twice in the chest.

As if on cue, Doc Bernstein emerged from the building with a bodybag, and headed straight to the van. He never looked up to make eye contact with me, the media, or anyone else for that matter.

I started to lunge toward him, but was thwarted by more agents. I could feel Anna and Billings immediately at my side holding me up, but the weight of the sorrow was too much to bear. I fell to my knees and began sobbing. He wasn't the best brother, but he was mine.

I knew that I had to be the one to tell Mom and Dad before they heard it on the news.

After tending to Anna's cuts, we all filed into the car and Billings drove us to the station. I would call them from my desk.

CHAPTER 23

The Somber Effects of Death

Anna

I never thought by the end of this fiasco I would be comforting John, instead of the other way around. I also never thought this would end in another death. First Tess, now Scott. I'm wary of this mystery-solving lifestyle. Maybe I need to lay low for a while…from everything: life, writing, book events, you name it.

It was a long, silent ride to the station and my cuts were starting to sting a bit. I'd better put some more ointment on when I get home. But for now, I'd have to suffer through it while I gave my statement to Billings.

The squad room was solemn and desolate when we walked in. Many of the officers came out to greet John and give their condolences. He just nodded and headed for his desk. I've never seen him so lifeless and monotone. To be honest, I've never seen him cry until today.

I glanced over my shoulder softly, smiling at him from across the room, as I followed Billings into the interrogation room. The recorder was started and I began to tell my tale of terror, which began at the coffee shop and ended in a war zone.

When I was done, Putnam walked me outside where John was waiting in the car and she drove us home. John and I held hands quietly in the back seat.

A half hour later, she pulled up to the house. "Just call me or Billings if you need anything at all, sir," Putnam said over her shoulder as we got out.

Surprisingly, the neighborhood was quiet and no one was waiting for us as we approached the front door. We opened the front door and the smell hit me right away. Full litter boxes. Ugh!

My babies seem to notice the sadness in the air and were softly purring while circling John and I in a slow rhythm.

"I'll take care of it, hun, why don't you just relax," I said.

"No, no, Anna, my sweet. You're the one who's been through hell, you go ahead and lay down."

John was so considerate and I knew even more so, in that moment, how lucky I was. I headed to the bathroom to run a bath and soak for a while.

I was drifting off surrounded by lavender scented candles and bubbles when John came in and sat on the edge of the tub. Even though it was dark, I could see Liza and Bette sneak in behind him, milling around my heap of clothes on the floor.

"How's my favorite girl?"

"Much better now."

"You know, Anna, one kidnapping was enough, but two kidnappings…" he paused to compose himself. "All of this is just too much for me to handle at once. I'm just glad I have you in my life – now more than ever."

I could see the tear forming in the corner of his eye. His lower lip was quivering slightly.

"No way you're getting rid of me that easily, Detective. I'm here for the long haul," I said as lifted my hand out of the water and placed it on top of his.

"I know you're parents are handling the arrangements, but I would really like to have everyone over after we leave the cemetery."

"My parents would like that, thanks. Now, how about we get you out of those suds and into bed?"

I never knew what it meant to have someone "give me butterflies" until I met John. But then, as I stared into his eyes and grinned like a schoolgirl, I knew. I knew that I would never have that feeling with anyone else, for as long as I live.

* * *

It was a beautiful ceremony, first at the church and then at the cemetery in Hamilton. A double ceremony for Tess and Scott. Tess's family was there, along with Scott's entire family, and few neighborhood friends, and many officers from John's precinct. It was a rough morning for me and I was running a bit late and hadn't formally met everyone yet, but would see them all at the house.

Since my house was fairly small, only close family and friends were coming back afterwards. It was a beautiful day, so we had the inside set up, along with a large tent in the yard with chairs and tables.

I had spent most of the day cooking and baking, while John cleaned up and set up the tent.

Tess's sister, Brittany, and her mother, were the first to arrive. I embraced her at the door and expressed my condolences again. She motioned her hand to a timid woman beside her and introduced her as Mary Ellen. I shook her hand and smiled, and she nodded in kind and thanked me for taking care of all the arrangements.

I knew the young girl with long brown hair and purple sundress, who was hiding slightly behind her mother, as Brittany's younger sister, Kat.

"And, you must be Kat. It's so nice to meet you. I saw your pretty pictures on Facebook."

"Yes ma'am, thank you. Um…are all these cats yours?" she asked shyly.

It seemed Petra and Tiny had taken a liking to her. Kat had bent down to rub their heads. She didn't know what she was getting into. Now they would follow her around all day.

"Yes, they are all my babies. And, I think they like you," I winked, while smiling softly.

I directed them to the tables John had set up and went back to the kitchen to finish setting up the lunch meat platter and Italian pasta salad bowl.

My back was to the doorway when John called me to come to the door. I wiped my hands and rushed to see what the fuss was about.

"John, dear, you know I'm right in the middle of fixing the —" I stopped mid-sentence. I recognized them from their photos and, of course, our once-in-a-blue-moon video calls.

"Anna, honey, I want you to meet my parents."

I was about to say what a pleasure it was to meet them, although under such somber circumstances, and shake their hand. However, they had other plans, and before I could extend my hand, Frank and Esther Solace snatched me up in a group embrace. They squeezed me tight and rubbed my back, telling me how happy they were their son found me.

The awkward moment lasted about ninety seconds, but felt more like an hour. I showed them to the tables out back and went back to the kitchen to fetch the food. John was there when I walked in, grinning from ear to ear. I rolled my eyes and smiled back.

"You can't say I never warned you," he chuckled.

"No, I can't. Now, wipe that smirk off your face and help with these platters. We have guests to comfort."

"Yes, dear."

A couple of hours later, the families were still sitting around eating and drinking, swapping stories about Tess and Scott. It was sad, but happy, at the same time. The whole thing was so surreal that I felt like they would walk through the door at any minute and yell, "Surprise, we got you! It was all a joke!" But, I knew it was real. Death was real. It comes suddenly, shakes up your life, and leaves a deep void that nothing can fill. I could feel John clinging tighter to me, more than ever, because of the void left by his brother's death. And that's fine with me. I'll be there for him, just like I'm there for Shirlene…my two best friends.

Speaking of Shirlene, it's strange that she hasn't returned my calls. I mean, I know she is on her fancy cruise with her new gentleman friend, but she could at least text back.

I turned my attention back to my guests and fetched another bottle of wine. It was going to be a long night.

* * *

A week after the funeral, John was back to work, trying to stay busy. I decided to head upstairs and clear out Scott's belongings from the apartement. As I was pulling the clothes from a drawer, an envelope fell out onto the floor. It wasn't sealed, so I opened it. It was dated a year ago. In short, it said , "If anything happens to me, ask the FBI why they failed me."

That's strange. What does the FBI have to do with anything? This note made me think Scott was involved with the FBI *before* he started the side job with LOV. I'd better keep this to myself. John has been through enough.

I tucked the letter in my pocket, grabbed the bags of Scott's clothing and other items, and headed back downstairs to finally email my mother back. I usually don't have much to say, but this time, there was a lot to report from the quiet suburbs of Princeton.

CHAPTER 24

Saying Goodbye from the Grave

Scott

It was the day of my and Tess's funeral. I was sitting in a dark, government-style SUV in between two suits watching the family I love in pain through tinted windows from down the street. I begged them to stop by the cemetery, but they refused. They finally gave in and parked down the street from Anna's house, so that I can have one more look at everyone. I never thought it would be so difficult to look at everyone so sad and in so much pain. I wish there was another way, but the FBI had to make it look like I was dead and gone forever. I had no idea that LOV had ties to the mafia in Newark and New York, and that they had put a hit out on me for the book.

All that time as an informant for the FBI was just not enough evidence to take all of the key players down, just the small players at the Hamilton facility. Apparently, there was someone else even higher up the food chain that ran the whole organization. He was the one that ordered the hit on me.

Now, I was stuck in the witness protection program for god-knows-how-long. At the very least, until the trial of Vanessa and Oscar Santiago is over, and the FBI can somehow get inside the mafia organization and eliminate the head guy.

I'm so sorry, Tess. I loved you so very much. But my whole life has been one failure after the next. I truly thought I was doing the right thing by arranging to do a few favors for LOV and pay back my debt, until I realized they were into more than just helping those in need of an organ transplant. They were taking innocent lives in the process.

When the FBI first approached me, I really wanted to help, and thought I was doing the right thing by agreeing to put the bad guys away. However, that didn't do anything but get my girlfriend killed and my brother's girlfriend kidnapped. The FBI made the offer sound so good when they approached me. They promised me exoneration, full immunity, and a big fat check for $10,000. Boy, was I stupid.

Until next time, big brother. I'm sure going to miss Anna's cooking.

CHAPTER 25

Champagne for Everyone!

Anna

It's been a few weeks since the funeral and I thought it would be a good idea to have a little get-together to lift John's spirits. Sometimes being around friends and loved ones can help. I have to admit, I'm a bit worried about John. He's been taking on a lot of overtime and double shifts at work and I hardly see him anymore.

I've invited Billings and Putnam, Mr. Craigly, my friend Bonnie from the newspaper, and her husband, Dave. They needed a break from their newborn and it was their first time leaving the baby with a sitter, which happened to be her mother.

Since it was a late evening gathering, I decided to keep the menu simple; just some hors d'oeuvres and a little chicken marsala. I set up the large table in the kitchen area with an extra six chairs, and hoped no one decided to bring a guest.

I called to John from the kitchen asking if he was dressed yet. There was no reply, but he shuffled into the kitchen a minute later asking me what I needed.

"Don't you look handsome this evening," I said flirtatiously.

"Why thank you, rosebud. Is that a new blouse?"

"It sure is. I can't believe you noticed."

John was so good about making me feel special, even when he was going through something himself. I was actually wearing blue jeans with my new, long-sleeve, button-up blouse. It was white with huge pink roses on it. And, on my feet, cute pink, low heel, strappy slip-ons.

I handed John the tablecloth, and pointed to the trays so he can start setting the table, while I fetched the wine, beers, and sodas.

"Everyone should be here in a few minutes, it's almost 7," I mentioned.

"Yeah. Although I don't know why you invited the neighborhood grouch over."

"Be nice. He's a lonely old man. Plus he sent that beautiful arrangement and card to the funeral home for your brother."

"That's true, I guess."

As if on cue, I heard a light tapping on the back door and knew our first guest had arrived. Mr. Craigly could only get his scooter in through that entrance, since the front door had steps.

"Welcome, Mr. Craigly! So glad you could make it!"

I could hear John's eye's rolling from the next room.

"John, can you help, please?"

John helped him in through the sliding glass doors.

"Thank you, Detective. Uh…I hope you don't mind, but I have a date coming in a bit."

John and I both stopped in our tracks and looked at each other. I finally broke the awkward silence.

"Sure, sure, that's fine. I'll just go add another chair at the table."

I could sense John silently giving him a high five in his head. It's a male thing, I don't know.

I was setting up the extra chair when the doorbell rang. It was the rest of the guests – Billings, Putnam, Bonnie, and Dave. After all of the introductions had been made, we moved into the living room for hors d'oeuvres – stuffed mushrooms with a spinach and feta filling and a cheese, pepperoni, and cracker platter.

The room was filled with lighthearted banter and laughter. It was nice to see John smile and laugh.

118

We were all in shock when Ms. Martinez from across the street showed up twenty minutes later. Especially when she announced she was Mr. Craigly's date! Ms. Martinez took a seat next to him and he put his arm around her and snuggled closer. She let out a giggle like a schoolgirl with a crush. It was so adorable. Things must be heating up between those two.

I called everyone for dinner with the clink of a fork to my wine glass, and the table soon filled up. I tried a new recipe for the chicken marsala, it was a white wine mushroom sauce with diced potatoes and red peppers.

John shared comical stories about him and his brother over dinner and managed to get in a few murder mysteries from cold cases as well. Of course, he had to answer questions from the curious Mr.Craigly about crime scenes and forensic science, who claims he needed the information for his very important work as a neighborhood watch captain.

It was a wonderful evening full of fun, laughter, and friends. It was actually the first time Ms. Martinez said more than a few words to me. She usually just frowns at me and points. But, she proved to me tonight that she was a pleasant woman with four children and six grandchildren. It was wonderful to hear, but we were all happy when she ran out of photos to show us on her phone.

After dinner, we served cheesecake with fresh strawberries and coffee. Everyone was eating and talking amongst themselves, even though they all said they couldn't eat another bite. John was next to me at the counter helping me with the dishes, when he dropped some silverware.

"Whoops, I'll get it."

"No! I mean, no, I got it rosebud."

John was acting a bit strange since dessert. I went back to the dishes, but noticed he was still on the floor. When I looked down, he was on one knee looking up at me. I asked what was wrong and that's when he presented a small box in his palm.

Everyone gasped, including me, and held their breath waiting for what was to come next.

He talked about how the death of his brother made him think about his mortality and that life was too short, and then he said it.

"Anna, will you marry me?" he said as he opened the small velvet box and revealed the most beautiful diamond I'd ever seen.

John wants to marry me, I said to myself. I was speechless at first, and then I was crying, and then I was feverishly nodding yes.

As John slipped the ring on my finger, I could not help but think how huge the diamond was and how all my married friends would be so thrilled for me. The biological clock has officially stopped. I could see Bonnie texting on her phone out the side of my eye. She had to spread the word! Ha!

Everyone stood around gawking at the ring, shaking John's hand and patting him on the back, while me and Putnam hugged.

"So, how does it feel to be engaged, Anna?" Ms. Martinez asked me. She had moved next to me, leaning in for a closer look at the ring. Standing with one hand on her hip she put on the glasses hanging from the chain around her neck and squinted. I knew the ring met her approval when she nodded vigorously and gave me a thumbs up.

A large pop startled me and I turned around to see John holding a bottle of champagne.

"Champagne for everyone!" he exclaimed.

As if on queue, Tiny and Bette jumped up on their hind legs to 'hug' John, while the others circled him. They remained on his legs until he bent down and acknowledged them.

That makes it official, he's a member of the family.

An hour or so later, we walked everyone outside and said our goodbyes. John and I were on the front step waving and noticed Mr. Craigly was headed to Ms. Martinez's house. When he turned around to wave goodnight, I could have sworn he winked.

When Billings and Putnam pulled off, I turned to John and asked about the policies on dating another fellow officer.

"Well, the captain hasn't said anything yet. So, I guess we'll see."

"Yep. But there is definitely some serious chemistry between those two! You never know…"

"Anna Romano, are you instigating a double wedding?" he bellowed, and then laughed aloud.

We headed inside still laughing and recapping the night's highlights as we cleaned up.

I was slipping under the covers ready to fall into a deep sleep when I thought about Shirlene again. I grabbed my phone off the nightstand and checked my screen. No messages or missed calls. Hmmm. I think the boat was supposed to dock early this evening. That's really not like her at all. I'll call the agency tomorrow when I wake up and see what they know. I just can't rest easy until I know my friend was okay.

I gently put my arm around John and smiled as I tried to drift off to sleep.

Prologue: Book 4

Anna

I could not believe what the agency just said to me. There had to be some kind of mistake. I sat there on the couch frowning, with my mouth partially agape.

John walked into the room and stopped in his tracks when he saw my face. It was the first Saturday he had off in months and wanted to go out for a special brunch to celebrate our engagement.

"Anna, are you okay? What's wrong?" he asked.

"No one has heard from or seen Shirlene since the before she left on the cruise. You know Shirlene. She doesn't just NOT answer her phone or texts. I'm afraid something is really wrong, John."

"Now now, let's not jump to conclusions, rosebud. What do you know about this man she went off with?"

"Nothing really. Just that he's wealthy, handsome and loved to spoil her. I should have pressed her for more information. This is all my fault!" I cried out in desperation.

"This is not your fault. Let me do some digging after we get back from brunch, okay?"

"Brunch. How can you think of food at a time like this? My best friend is missing from a cruise ship!"

"Okay, dear. Email me the cruise ship information and the agency's number, and I'll get right on it. Meanwhile, I'll be in kitchen making a sandwich."

"Thank you so much, John. What would I do without you?"

I shooed Jasmine from my keyboard and Sonny from my chair and started gathering the information John needed.

After hitting *Send*, I decided to check my email. There were several from the newspaper reminding me to respond to the latest letters from readers who need help with their various personal and professional problems for my Dear Jesse column. And, there was one from my mom, wanting to know why she had to hear about my engagement from Bonnie. The last email had no subject, and I was about to drag it to the junk folder, when I read the body of the email. All it said was 'Murder at Sea'. I froze for a moment, then stood up and slowly walked to the bookshelf. I looked up at the top shelf and found the book I was looking for. The title was glaring back at me, as if to mock me. *Murder at Sea* by Anna Romano.

It was one of my earlier books when I first started writing and only had two cats. It was about a man who murdered his new bride on the ship and then got off when the ship docked without a trace. He had proposed to the woman on the ship, had a private ceremony perfomed by the captain, and then created the illusion that she was with him all along by having his accomplice dress up in her clothes. That way he had witnesses who would attest to seeing them around the ship and getting off the ship together. Meanwhile, the bride was hidden somewhere on the ship in a locked, confined space, and the cops only had 72 hours to find her before her oxygen ran out. But, the woman in my book was secretly an heir to a family fortune and he stood to gain a large inheritance if she died. Shirlene doesn't have anything like that, does she? And how would he have known anyway?

I was reaching up, pulling the book from the shelf, when John walked in with a fried egg sandwich, dripping egg yolk down the front of his shirt.

"What have you got there?" he asked.

"Possibly, the first clue to Shirlene's disappearance."

With a creased forehead, John asked what I meant. I showed him the email and gave him a summary of the book.

"Okay, Anna, I'm going to stop you right here. This is now officially a suspicious disappearance, and I DON'T want you involved. Understood?"

"But, she's MY best friend, John! You can't expect me to sit back and do nothing!" I shouted. It was the first time I had raised my voice at John and he was taken aback.

"I know she is your friend. She is a good friend to both of us. Let me take the information you sent me and do some investigating. I've already texted Billings to open a missing person's case for Shirlene. You think you can sit tight for a few hours while I meet with Billings at the station?"

I nodded yes and plopped onto the couch, reaching for the remote.

"I'll also have the tech guy come over here within the hour to try and trace to source of the email, so be sure to listen for the door."

I nodded again and turned my attention back to my home improvement show.

The door shut behind him and my mind quickly switched gears. I was thinking about how to get access to Shirlene's dating site credentials, so I can find out who this mystery man was. There was only one nosy, techy person I knew of who I could trust to help.

I walked over to the computer and pulled up my messaging app and clicked on her ID, cathym69.

I sat and waited for Chatty Cathy Morton to respond.

About the Author

Cheryl Denise Bannerman, is a multi-genre author of six self-published books and winner of the 2018 Book Excellence Award for her book of poetry, Words Never Spoken.

Within the author's first three works of fiction, Black Child to Black Woman, Words Never Spoken, and A Killer's Reflection, the author addresses critical topics of social concern, such as alcohol and drug addictions, racism and bigotry, domestic abuse and violence, suicide, and child molestation.

In her latest releases, a cozy mystery series entitled the Anna Romano Mystery Series, she hopes to provide relief from a somewhat somber world and spread laughter and smiles with the main character's witty humor and 'unintentional stumbling' over dead bodies and into murder investigations.

Her goal in life is to keep writing and continue helping victims of Domestic Abuse/Violence, Grief and ANON family groups, and Corporate Health and Wellness groups, to heal through words -- encouraging them to 'write the pain' via journaling, and expressing themselves through short stories, songs, and poetry.

She currently resides in Orlando, Florida, where she runs her 24-year-old Training and Development company, specializing in Instructional Design and eLearning.

In her spare time, she loves to read murder mysteries, attend museums, watch movies, try new cuisines, shop with her daughter, and take in the sun on the beach. And, although this author's works are fiction, she has incorporated many of her personal life's experiences into their stories.

Appendix of Tasty Recipes

Ricotta And Egg Gnocchi With Olives, Capers, And Tomato Sauce

Resource: https://www.saveur.com/article/recipes/ricotta-and-egg-gnocchi-with-olives-capers-and-tomato-sauce

INGREDIENTS

2 lb. medium Yukon Gold potatoes, scrubbed

1 ⅔ cups all-purpose flour, plus more for dusting

7 tbsp. homemade ricotta or store-bought whole-milk ricotta

2 tsp. kosher salt

2 eggs

Make the gnocchi: Boil potatoes in a 4-qt. saucepan of water. Reduce heat to medium-high; simmer until potatoes are tender, 25–30 minutes, and drain. When cool enough to handle, peel and pass the potatoes through a potato ricer into a bowl. Add flour, ricotta, salt, and eggs; using your hands, mix until a smooth dough forms. If dough is sticky, add more flour, 1 tbsp. at a time, as needed.

Transfer dough to a lightly floured surface; quarter dough. Working with one-quarter dough at a time, use your hands to roll dough into a ¾"-thick rope. Cut rope crosswise into 1" gnocchi; transfer to a flour-dusted, parchment paper—lined baking sheet. Separate gnocchi to prevent sticking. Cover with plastic wrap; chill until ready to cook.

FOR THE SAUCE

2 tbsp. extra-virgin olive oil, plus more for drizzling

1/2 tsp. crushed red chile flakes

4 cloves garlic, minced

1 bay leaf

1 medium yellow onion, minced

1 sprig rosemary

6 tbsp. unsalted butter, cubed

2 (28-oz.) cans whole peeled tomatoes, crushed by hand

Kosher salt and freshly ground black pepper, to taste

3/4 cup pitted green Castelvetrano or Gaeta olives, pitted and halved

1/3 cup finely grated Pecorino Romano, plus more for serving

1/4 cup capers, rinsed and roughly chopped

2 tbsp. roughly chopped wild or regular oregano

Make the sauce and serve: Heat oil in a 6-qt. saucepan over medium. Cook chile flakes, garlic, bay leaf, onion, and rosemary until vegetables are soft, 6–8 minutes. Add butter, tomatoes, and salt; simmer until thickened, about 1 1/2 hours. Discard bay leaf and rosemary; keep sauce warm. Bring a large pot of generously salted water to a simmer over medium-high. Cook gnocchi, all at once, until they float, 2–3 minutes. Stir olives, pecorino, capers, and oregano into sauce. Using a slotted spoon, transfer gnocchi to sauce; season with salt and pepper and stir to combine. Divide gnocchi between serving bowls; drizzle with olive oil and sprinkle with pecorino.

Spagetti Puttanesca

Resource: https://www.epicurious.com/recipes/food/views/
spaghetti-alla-puttanesca-241131

INGREDIENTS

1/4 cup extra-virgin olive oil

4 large garlic cloves, finely chopped

1 28.2-ounce can peeled tomatoes in puree with basil

1/2 cup Kalamata olives, halved, pitted

3 anchovy fillets, chopped

1 1/2 tablespoons drained capers

1 teaspoon dried oregano

1/2 teaspoon dried crushed red pepper

3/4 pound spaghetti

2 tablespoons chopped fresh Italian parsley

Grated Parmesan cheese

PREPARATION

Heat oil in large pot over medium heat. Add garlic and sauté until fragrant, about 1 minute. Add tomatoes with puree, olives, anchovies, capers, oregano, and crushed red pepper. Simmer sauce over medium-low heat until thickened, breaking up tomatoes with spoon, about 8 minutes. Season with salt and pepper.

Meanwhile, cook pasta in large pot of boiling salted water until tender but still firm to bite. Drain pasta; return to same pot. Add sauce and parsley. Toss over low heat until sauce coats pasta, about 3 minutes. Serve with cheese.

Cannoli Recipe With Pistacchio

Resource: https://www.vincenzosplate.com/recipe-items/
cannoli-recipe-pistacchio/

INGREDIENTS FOR PASTRY:

1 tsp cinnamon

1 tsp choc powder/cocoa

1 tsp table salt

1 tsp ground coffee

1 egg

1 tsp icing suguar

250g plain flour

30ml white vinegar

30ml Marsala (this can be difficult to find so you can
replace it with Amaretto or Frangelico)

50g lard

Peanut Oil (for frying)

INGREDIENTS FOR FILLING:

3 egg yolks

90g sugar

80g flour

120gr of Pistachio nuts (unsalted)

500ml milk

3-5 tablespoons of extra virgin olive oil (EVOO)

UTENSILS:

2 medium sized mixing bowls

Whisk

Electric Mixer

Fork

1 small saucepan

Small sized sieve

4 metal tubes for making cannoli (you will not be able to achieve the shell shape without this!)

Cookie cutter (9cm in diameter)

Pastry bag (Or a zip lock bag if you don't have one!)

CANNOLI RECIPE STEP ONE – PREPARING THE PASTRY:

Sift the flour into a mixing bowl, then add the salt, cocoa, coffee powder, icing sugar and cinnamon.

Next, add the lard.

Break the egg into the bowl and mix everything together really well using your hands.

Adding just a small amount at a time, pour in the Marsala & white wine vinegar, and mix it through. Do this gradually to make sure the dough remains soft and firm, and you might reach the consistency you need without adding all of these liquids.

Add a small amount of flour to your work bench an continue to knead the dough on top..

All of your ingredients should have come together at this point and it will feel a bit harder than bread dough.

Wrap it in cling film (glad wrap) and leave it in the fridge for 1 hour.

CANNOLI RECIPE STEP TWO – PREPARING THE FILLING:

Mix egg yolks with 90g sugar using an electric hand mixer for the Italian Canolli with pistachio cream.

Add 50g flour and 100ml of milk and stir using a low speed until the flour dissolves.

Warm up 400ml of milk on a low heat.

Crush the pistachio nuts using a blender then use a mortar and pestle to mix with 2-3 tablespoons of EVOO.

Once the milk is warm (not boiling), add the pistachio and use the electric mixer on a low speed to combine.

Add the egg mixture and continue to combine while the saucepan is still on heat until it becomes beautiful and creamy.

TIP: Add a small amount of additional flour if the cream is too runny.

Transfer the cream into a bowl and seal the bowl with glad wrap making sure it completely covers the top of the cream so no air can get in.

Put the cream in the fridge for at least an hour and fry up the canolli shells!

FRYING THE CANNOLI SHELLS:

Remove the dough from the fridge and cut a piece from the end.

Add some flour to the work bench, place the dough in the centre, and begin to spread it out into a circle using a rolling pin. It should be no more than 1-2mm thick.

Using a round cookie cutter, cut out a circle, then lift it out and wrap it around one of the metal tubes until the ends meet and join the two together using a small amount of egg white.

Repeat this, covering all of the metal tubes.

Once the oil has reached 170-180°C, drop in two shells at a time, and allowing them to cook for around 2 minutes. Keep an eye on them, they should be brown but not burnt!

TIP: If you try to fry more than two at a time, the oil will start to cool down and you won't get a good result!

Only once the shells have completely cooled (this will take around 20 minutes), remove the metal tube and now they are ready to be filled!

HOW TO SERVE

The shells should only be filled just before you serve or they won't stay crispy! When it is time for dessert, fill a pastry bag with the pistachio cream, squeezing it into the tubes, getting enough on both sides.

TIP: If you don't have a pastry bag, just fill a small zip lock bag with the cream, and cut off one of the corners.

Dust a generous amount of icing sugar over the top using a small sieve.

What Did You Think of Family Ties, Missing Organs, & Champagne?

First, thank you for purchasing this book, *Family Ties, Missing Organs, & Champagne*. I know you could have picked any number of books to read, but you picked this book, and for that, I am extremely grateful.

I hope that it added value and quality to your everyday life. If so, it would be awesome if you could share this book with your friends and family by posting to social media.

If you enjoyed this book and found some benefit in reading this, I would like to hear from you and hope that you could take some time to post a review online. Your feedback and support will help me to greatly improve my writing craft for future projects and make this book even better.

Visit the web site at www.bannermanbooks.com for contact information.

I want you, the reader, to know that your opinion is very important to me and hope that you will check out my other works of fiction:

Title	*Category/Genre*
Cats, Cannolis, and a Curious Kidnapping	*Book 1 of the Anna Romano Mystery Series*
A Bloody Stiletto, Cold Lasagna, and a Bestseller	*Book 2 of the Anna Romano Mystery Series*
Words Never Spoken	*Women's Inspirational/Poetry*
A Killer's Reflection	*Erotic Psychological Thriller/Serial Killer*
Black Child to Black Woman	*Women's Fiction/Urban Fiction/Family Saga*